TOTAL WAR

REED MONTGOMERY BOOK 3

LOGAN RYLES

SEVERN RIVER PUBLISHING

Severn River Publishing
SevernRiverBooks.com

ISBN: 978-1-64875-538-5 (Paperback)

ALSO BY LOGAN RYLES

For my parents, Tony and Karen,

who taught me the spirit of a pioneer.

1

"Are you here to check in?"

The woman behind the counter wore a red velvet vest, black satin pants, and shoes that gleamed under the casino lights. Her hair was knotted behind her head, exposing the tight skin of too many facelifts and not enough vitamin D. The smile she wore couldn't hide the exhaustion in her eyes or the disinterest in her tone.

Reed pushed his aviator sunglasses closer to his eyes. He laid the metal business card on the counter, and the casino lights glinted off its glossy black surface, shining on the emblem of a silver badger etched in the center of the card.

"I'm here to see Mr. Muri."

A shadow of emotion broke the exhaustion in her vacant gaze. Or maybe it was excitement. Trepidation?

They so often look the same. I wonder if she knows what kind of man she works for.

The woman smiled again, nodded once, and disappeared through a doorway. Reed replaced the card into his pocket and leaned against the counter. The edge of the granite bit into the back of his sport coat, colliding with his bruised back. Through the dark lenses of his sunglasses, the flashing neon lights were only partially muted. The *shrink* of slot machine levers melded with the clinking ring of the dials as they spun like Ferris wheels on crack. A craps table on the far side of the room was crowded by a dozen men in collared shirts, half-drunk, leaning in and shouting as the dice bounced over the scarlet felt. The faint odor of flowers wafted from an air freshening device buried in the vents of the overhead AC unit, a clever design that subdued the chaos and tension of the room and further facilitated reckless spending.

What a masterpiece. And people wonder why the house always wins.

"Sir?" The woman returned to the counter.

Reed stood up with a soft grunt as his aching muscles objected to the movement. Her smile was gone now. Two large men with emotionless stares accompanied her, both dressed in dark grey suits that bulged around oversized arms and barrel chests.

Why do all mob goons look the same?

"These men will escort you to Mr. Muri."

Reed stepped around the counter. The first goon pushed the door open and led the way into a hall while the second fell in behind Reed. Flashes of orange and blue from the casino floor vanished into a sterile white of LED overheads glaring onto the floor and walls. The hall reminded Reed of a sick ward in a hospital—bare minimum in every way with plain metal doors and cheap linoleum flooring.

The house doesn't waste money, either. Another reason it always wins.

Except for today. Today, everyone would lose. It was why Reed left Georgia and drove twelve hours to be there. It was why he jacked himself up on caffeine pills before leaving the rental car in an alley and slipping up to the casino like another drunk tourist—casual, but fully alert and ready to kill.

Today the house will burn.

Twin silver doors blocked their path at the end of the hall. The lead goon punched a button on the wall, and the elevator opened immediately, revealing an interior decorated with mahogany panels and gold rails. Gentle elevator music drifted down from invisible speakers. Reed walked in and waited while the two men swiped ID cards. The doors glided shut, and they turned on him as the car began to descend.

"Arms up." The command was as blunt and bland as the man who grunted it. Reed lifted his arms while the men felt down his legs, around his waist, and over his ribcage. The big hand running up his side stopped at the suede holster with the oversized revolver tucked inside. The retainer strap clicked, and the weapon fell into the goon's fingers.

The men looked down at the massive handgun. Even with a short, four-inch barrel, the .500 magnum revolver dwarfed their large hands. As the first man lifted the gun and raised both eyebrows, the gaping, .50 caliber muzzle stared Reed in the face.

Reed shrugged. "Bear hunting."

They sneered at him, and the revolver disappeared beneath one man's sport coat as the elevator bell rang and the doors rolled open. Reed was shoved forward into a hallway that couldn't have been more different from the stark white of four floors above. More mahogany panels framed dark red carpet, gold trim, and brass light fixtures. Shadows clung to the corners, and the big feet of the two men behind him barely made a sound as they propelled him down the hallway toward the tall oak door at the end. Both men placed their thumbs against a black panel mounted next to the door-jamb, and the lock clicked.

This Muri guy really thinks he's something. All middlemen do.

The door swung open without a sound, and once more, the meaty hands pushed him forward. Reed stumbled across the carpet onto a thick rug, his vision temporarily blinded by the flash of lights overhead. Built into the walls of the large room were tall bookshelves, and a giant leather couch faced him next to a glass table stacked with liquor bottles. A quick survey of the occupants revealed a tall, thin man in a suit standing in one corner, a whiskey glass in one hand and his black hair plastered against his scalp. Only one other person occupied the parlor, and he faced Reed from the comfort of the oversized leather couch, one leg crossed over the other and round glasses mounted over a pointed nose. His face was worn and pale, with a network of scars tracing his left cheek and leading up to his ear.

Reed heard the door click behind him, and he tugged at the bottom of his jacket, brushing out the wrinkles left by the thick fingers of the two goons. One thug handed the revolver to the man on the couch, who surveyed the weapon, then motioned toward a chair sitting across from him. Reed adjusted his sunglasses again, then took a seat.

"Welcome." The man's voice was smooth, laden with a thick Swiss accent, but he spoke with the relaxed tone of a person comfortable with English. "Charles, won't you pour our guest a brandy?"

The tall man with the black hair lifted a bottle of brown liquor, then handed Reed a tumbler textured with diamond stipples. The first sip revealed the unmistakable smoky smoothness of a high-dollar brand—something old and rare.

"Thank you." Reed lifted the glass toward the man on the couch and was answered with a slight bow.

"Whom do I have the pleasure of hosting?" The voice was still calm, but an air of directness slipped into the tone.

Reed set the glass on the table and popped his knuckles. "Call me Chris. It's not overly important who I am."

The man shrugged—slight and disinterested. "Fine. What can I do for you, *Chris?*"

"I understand you're in the business of brokering contractors. Specifically, the criminal kind."

The room fell silent. Reed was vaguely aware of the two big men standing to his left, and Charles stepped behind a tall armchair, his hands falling out of sight.

Probably to a gun or a knife. As if either will save him.

The man on the couch smiled. "You're quite mistaken. I'm a simple businessman. A casino owner. Nothing more."

Reed leaned back in the chair and crossed his legs. He flipped the card from his pocket and onto the coffee table between them, then returned the smile. "No, you're not. You're Cedric Muri. The goon broker."

The smile on Cedric's face faded as he eyed the card with the glowing silver badger. He took a long sip of brandy, then returned his gaze to Reed. "Where did you get that?"

"From a dead man. Big fellow, cross-eyed. Carried a rather large Smith & Wesson revolver. The one you're holding, as it happens."

Cedric's gaze fell to the weapon, then returned to Reed. Fire blazed in his eyes, and he dropped the brandy onto the coffee table. He sat forward. "Why are you here?"

"We'll get to that in just a moment. First, I need some information. Besides the big guy I killed in North Carolina, you also hired out some East European thugs to a South American prick named Salvador. While I was busy carving them up in Atlanta, one of them mentioned your name. So, my question is, why are you supplying soldiers to the people who want to kill me?"

Cedric's lips lifted into a smile. "Reed Montgomery. The assassin."

Reed nodded. "That's me, although I'm trying my damnedest to retire. People like you are making it difficult."

"That's because people like me are threatened by rogue assassins like you."

"You wouldn't be if you had stayed out of it. Those two Europeans I mentioned kidnapped a young lady on behalf of Mr. Salvador. I happen to like her a lot. And then, of course, there are the men I gunned down at Pratt-Pullman Yard in Atlanta. None of these shitheads were proper soldiers. None of them were Oliver Enfield's men. So they must've been yours, and you're going to tell me who paid for them."

Cedric drummed the tips of his fingers against each other, producing the only noise in the still room. He lifted one finger and motioned toward Reed. "I think we're done here, Mr. Montgomery. I'm sure Mr. Salvador will pay handsomely for your head."

Reed lifted the brandy glass and drained the contents. "I was hoping you'd say that."

The floor creaked under the weight of one of the big men, whose reflection Reed saw flash in the gold railing behind Cedric. As he leaned forward to deliver a death blow, Reed sprang from the chair, and without turning around, grabbed him by the arm. With a quick heave, he bent forward and dragged him over his back. The goon sailed over the chair and crashed against the tabletop in an explosion of glass. A gunshot cracked from behind Reed, snapping against the wooden walls and reverberating in his ears. Cedric dove to the carpet as Reed followed him, and Charles vanished behind the minibar.

The revolver's grip filled Reed's hands as he jerked it off the floor and spun it toward the thug lying amid the shattered table. With a quick pull of the trigger, the room erupted into an explosion. The man on the floor convulsed as his head was blasted apart under the smashing impact of the 350-grain projectile. The shockwave that tore through Reed's arm sent him hurtling back against the floor as though a horse had kicked him. Glass tore through his jacket and into his shoulder, sinking into flesh so bruised he barely felt the cuts. Reed redirected the revolver and fired again, sending the second goon crashing to the floor.

Two more shots tore through the paneling that sheltered Charles, sending shards of wood spraying over the floor amid the broken liquor bottles. The gunshots ceased. Reed picked himself up, rubbing a sore shoulder. The handgun kicked like nothing he'd ever fired before. His hand ached, and his ears rang from the thunderous blast.

But it damn sure gets the job done.

The two fallen gunmen lay still and silent, with none of the twitches or residual fighting power he was used to men having after he shot them in the chest with his 9mm. The Smith & Wesson 500 was the cannon of the handgun world. The last word.

A gasping, rasping sound leaked from behind the couch. Reed rubbed his thumb against the Smith and shoved the couch out of the way, exposing the groveling figure of Cedric Muri on the floor behind it. Slobber and spilled brandy coated the hardwood floor beneath him, and he scrambled backward as Reed advanced.

"You should've worked with me, Cedric."

"Please . . ." Cedric held out his hand. "Let's discuss this!"

Reed squatted on the carpet and grabbed Cedric by the hair, pulling him forward and shoving the Smith's muzzle against his neck. Patience and self-restraint vanished from his body as renewed rage replaced them, quickening his heart rate and making his hand shake against the handle of the gun.

"Listen to me, you *shit*. Last week, a house burned down in Canton, Georgia. Two people died. Were your men involved?"

Cedric choked and struggled against the gun. "I don't know!"

Reed shoved the gun harder into his throat. "Like hell you don't know. *Tell me!*"

"I swear I never know what my men are hired to do! I'm just a business—"

Reed smashed the revolver against the side of Cedric's skull. "No more excuses! Do I look like I care?"

Once more, Cedric clawed at Reed's arm and tried to look away.

Reed slammed his head back against the couch and screamed into his face. "*Look at me like a man when I'm talking to you!*"

Cedric shuddered, then slowly turned his head toward Reed.

"Were your men responsible? Answer the question."

Reed had stared into a lot of eyes in the moments preceding a kill. Sometimes those eyes were a hundred yards away, viewed through a scope. Sometimes they were only photos—images of the people he was hunting. In none had he seen such total terror like the complete, consuming fear that filled Cedric's.

The shuddering fragment of a man on the floor nodded his confession.

Reed threw Cedric against the floorboards and stood up. "Do you know her name?"

Cedric just sobbed.

"I thought not. Her name was Kelly Armstrong, and she was a good woman. I don't suppose you know what that means, but it's an incredibly rare thing to find anyone good in this world. Kelly was the best of the best. Your men torched her house and burned her alive."

Reed lifted the revolver and opened the cylinder. He ejected the spent .50 caliber casings, then fed new cartridges into the weapon. Cedric gasped for air, his wide eyes fixed on the handgun.

"Do you know what they call me?" Reed snapped the cylinder shut and faced Cedric. "I know you've heard. What's my name?"

Cedric's voice warbled over the bile that boiled out of his throat. "They call you The Prosecutor."

"That's right. They call me the prosecutor—because I'm all about justice. I lay down the law, balance the scales. Or at least that's what I told myself, so I could sleep at night. But all that has changed. I'm over it, you know? I've moved on to bigger things. So you can rest assured I'm not a prosecutor, and I'm not here for justice."

Momentary hope flashed in Cedric's eyes as he peered up at Reed, his fingernails sinking into the hardwood. That hope vanished the instant Reed laid the muzzle against Cedric's forehead and cocked the hammer.

"I'm an executioner. And I'm here for revenge."

"No . . . please . . ." New sobs escaped Cedric's throat as he stared down the barrel and into Reed's cold eyes.

"Who hired you?" Reed spat out the question like a bad taste in his mouth. "Was it Enfield?"

Cedric shook his head.

"So, who was it? Give me a name, and I'll make your death quick."

"Please . . . don't kill me. I have a family."

"*So did she!*" Reed screamed and kicked Cedric in the stomach. The man fell forward, coughing and spluttering over the carpet.

"*Who are they?*"

"I don't know. I never had a name. I only dealt with Salvador."

Reed gripped the revolver, wondering if he could believe Cedric, then decided that it didn't matter. "I should kill you. You deserve to die. Do you know that?"

Cedric convulsed on the floor and didn't answer.

Reed grabbed him by the hair and screamed in his face. "I said, *do you know that?*"

Tears streamed down his face as Cedric nodded. "Yes . . . yes. I do. I deserve to die."

Reed released him and spat on the floor. "I'm glad we're on the same page. It just so happens I'm going to let you live, because you have a job to do. Do you understand me?"

Cedric nodded emphatically. "What do you want?"

"I want them to know who's coming for them. I want them to know they rattled the wrong cage. Go back to your bosses and tell them Reed Montgomery has declared total war. Do you understand me?"

Cedric nodded again, sweat dripping off his sharp cheekbones.

Reed lowered the weapon, relaxing his finger off the trigger. He stared at the man on the floor, then walked away. Cedric gasped for air behind him, and Reed heard his hands hit the floor. A soft, metallic click echoed through the room.

In one fluid motion, Reed spun around, and the gun bucked in his hand as he pulled the trigger. The bullet smashed into Cedric's chest and sent him crashing to the floor as the pistol fell from his hands.

Reed holstered the revolver beneath his shirt and leered into the security camera on the ceiling. He lifted one hand and pointed into the lens. "I'm coming."

2

University of Edinburgh
Edinburgh, Scotland, United Kingdom

"A tradition of excellence in both academic achievement and the pursuits of human development is the most sacred value of this institution and has been since our founding. When calling to mind some of the greatest examples of students who have embraced these values over the course of my forty-year career, the young man who will speak next will most certainly be among the first names I remember. He is a sterling example of work ethic, dedication, and a relentless desire to push the barrier of knowledge as we know it. For the graduating class of Edinburgh Medical School, please welcome for the first time . . . Dr. Wolfgang Pierce!"

The old hall erupted in cheers from the hundreds of guests and students. Many of the voices that called out in excitement reflected accents from all over the world—Australian, Spanish, Indian, Polish—but the slender white male who mounted the steps was unmistakably American. With high cheekbones and a bold brow, his body language was consumed by overtones of excitement as he smiled at the crowd and waved at his fellow students. The spring in his step spoke to his youth—not more than thirty-five—but the quiet confidence that followed him as he stepped behind the podium felt older and more collected.

Wolfgang rested his hands on the worn mahogany. As the cheering died out, the hall was again swallowed in stillness and genuine anticipation, as though the guests in this hallowed place actually cared about what Wolfgang would say next. His fellow students knew him not just as the academic king of the university but as a friend—a smiling face with kind words for every class.

"Thank you, Dean Rostier. And thank you, ladies and gentlemen, for your generous welcome. My name is Wolfgang, and I'm from New York."

Before he could continue, another eruption of applause broke from the student body. He smiled warmly and nodded at them, waiting for the disruption to die out before he cleared his throat.

"I came to the University of Edinburgh after completing my graduate studies at Cambridge. Over the past three years, I have experienced the most sincere and overwhelming joy being a part of the outstanding program this university administers in the interest of advancing medical science. I consider myself to be amongst the most fortunate people in the world to have learned here and contributed to ongoing medical research. Today, as we gather to celebrate our achievements and prepare to take the next steps in our careers, I want to tell you a personal story. Something very dear to me."

The silence in the hallway was so perfect, Wolfgang could hear the softest breath in the back of the room. Excitement and nervousness warred with the practiced calm in his mind, threatening to overwhelm him. He didn't like crowds or stages, and he enjoyed delivering a speech even less than listening to one. But today was important—too important to worry about himself.

"As many of you know, somebody very special to me suffers from a terrible disease. Her name is Collins, and she's my twenty-year-old sister. From the time she was born, Collins has been a victim of the genetic disorder cystic fibrosis. It's a chronic disease that hampers a person's ability to breathe. Normal daily functions become a chore—strenuous physical activity becomes impossible. Although Collins should be enjoying the excitement of her sophomore year at college, she spends most of her days inside, plagued by painful coughs and a weak body. Worse still, her life expectancy is half the average of the western world."

Wolfgang hesitated as nervousness and emotion built in his chest, but he forced it back and wrapped his fingers around the edge of the podium.

"The amazing thing about Collins is that even though this disease has robbed so much from her, it hasn't touched her personality. She is a beautiful soul, with the sweetest and most generous temperament of any human I've ever met. She's an angel. We say that often about people who are dear to us, but truly, Collins is born straight from Heaven."

Wolfgang accepted a cup of water from a nearby professor and took a slow sip.

"My fellow graduates, we're not here for ourselves. We don't study and research and fight for breakthroughs to build our own résumés or add awards to our office desks. We're here because we all play a critical role in protecting the most precious thing on Earth—life itself. We all have a battle to fight, a mountain to climb, and a cause to champion. The best doctors and the finest scientists dedicate their every day to conquering those challenges and lifting those who are too weak to lift themselves. For me, my fight is cystic fibrosis, and my cause is the seventy thousand human beings around the world who suffer from it."

Wolfgang clenched his fist and rested it against the stand. His voice rose in tone, booming through the hall as he continued.

"Some will say that some dragons cannot be slain. Some mountains cannot be climbed. Some causes are lost. To these people, I have only this to say: If you won't join us, then stand back and watch us. Because we are the generation that *will* slay the dragon. They said smallpox couldn't be killed. Polio couldn't be healed. Soldiers with missing limbs could never walk again. The generations who came before us climbed those mountains, lifted us onto their shoulders, and now say to us that it is *our turn*. My fellow classmates, your fight begins today!"

Applause thundered against the wooden walls as the crowd stood and cheered. Wolfgang stepped away from the podium and offered a brief bow before shaking the dean's hand and smiling at his classmates. They smiled back with rosy cheeks, alive with the thrill and glory of the moment. He knew they felt like conquerors already. Most of them probably had no concept of the gravity of his words, which was precisely why he kept his remarks so brief. They probably wouldn't be willing to do what it took to reach those mountain peaks—or even begin the climb. But he was willing and able.

As the volume of the crowd increased, Wolfgang slipped through a door in the back of the hall and peeled off his graduation cap. He left it with the gown on an end table and adjusted his tie before stepping out into the brisk chill of the impending Scottish winter. He wouldn't miss Edinburgh, although he had hardly set foot on the campus over the last two years, anyway. It was time to head back to the States.

Twenty yards away from the hall, Wolfgang stopped under the skeleton shade of an elm tree and pulled his phone from his pocket. There was a missed call from an unknown number, but no voicemail. He hit redial and waited while it rang twice. Across the street, freshmen students walked between the old university buildings, knotted close together with their heads held low under the biting wind. They smiled and laughed, and the boys smacked each other on the arms. Wolfgang wondered if any of them took their studies as seriously as he did, if they understood the gravity of their role in this brief life.

Likely not.

"Wolfgang, I called you twice. Where the hell are you?"

The snapping voice on the phone was taut with the bluster of a man who felt out of control and wasn't used to it. His South American accent was hampered by anger, causing his mispronunciations of English words to become almost unintelligible.

"Salvador, I told you before. I don't tolerate profanity. We can speak to each other professionally, or not at all."

Salvador spluttered and then moderated his breathing. He spoke again, slower this time. "Very well, *Mr. Pierce*. Where are you?"

"Europe."

"*Europe?*" Salvador's voice cracked. "What the fu—"

Wolfgang hung up the phone. He retrieved a stick of gum from his pocket and chomped it between his teeth, flooding his mouth with mint as he resumed his surveillance of the passing freshmen. The boys still laughed and showed off while girls giggled and pretended to ignore them.

It was okay that they didn't take much seriously right now. Life was serious enough, and their days would come, but for now, they enjoyed the simple pleasures that Collins never had—of being young and free. In a way, this very trivialness was what he fought for.

The phone rang.

Wolfgang cleared his throat and spoke before Salvador could. "Listen to me carefully. I am a contractor, not an employee. Furthermore, I am disinclined to tolerate your primitive form of communication and will terminate our arrangement if you curse again. Are we clear?"

The breath whistled between Salvador's teeth. "You're an arrogant little snot, aren't you?"

"Hardly. I'm simply a man of self-respect who values the power of words. Now then, with regard to my present location. As a contractor, I am under no obligation to report to you my whereabouts or activities, and you will not challenge me on this issue again."

"As a *contractor,* you have a *contract,*" Salvador snarled. "Are you *reneging* on that contract, Mr. Pierce?"

"Points for the correct application of an excellent verb. No, I am not reneging on anything. I will kill Reed Montgomery. I just haven't done it yet. I pulled back in North Carolina because you assured me that Oliver Enfield and his men had things under control. It appears you were mistaken."

"What happened in North Carolina has no bearing on our contract. I want him killed, and I want him killed *now.*"

Wolfgang indulged in a tired sigh. "Very well. I'm headed back to the States. I'll start in Atlanta and keep you posted."

He ended the call before Salvador could add any last-minute outbursts. The students were gone now, and a taxi waited at the end of the street. Wolfgang slid into the back seat and smiled at the driver. "Edinburgh Airport, please."

3

Reed handed the Uber driver a twenty before stepping out of the Prius and into the warm sun. In stark contrast to the whistling wind and damp air of New Jersey, late fall was kind to Georgia. Orange and brown leaves skipped over the pavement, complementing the Christmas decorations adorning homes and businesses. The scent of dying vegetation and a dropping temperature drifted between the buildings and breathed fresh energy into his lungs—a welcome relief after months of a thick, humid summer.

The auto shop at the corner of two residential streets consisted of a block building with hand-painted letters advertising the services its owner provided. Half a dozen beater cars were parked out front, and the pop and click of a welder rang from the garage in the back. It looked like the kind of brake-swapping, oil-changing place that had been servicing cars since the roads around it were paved in dirt, but Reed wasn't fooled. Hidden behind the dirty blocks and dusty yard was a precision racing shop that rivaled NASCAR's best pits—a true hidden gem amid the bustling city.

Reed shouldered his backpack and stepped around the open gate into the fenced yard. The clicking of the welder was louder now, joined by the whine of an air wrench. Everything smelled of oil and grease—a scent Reed would buy a candle in if he could. He indulged in a brief smile, then ducked into the shop.

Mike Wooster looked up from his workbench when Reed slipped in. The big man was covered in grease up to his elbows and had smudges on his face. He wiped his hands on a cloth and shot Reed a wide smile. "Welcome back. I was about to call you."

Reed accepted the crushing handshake and glanced around the shop. A Corvette Z06 hung six feet off the ground on a lift, while a mechanic worked beneath it with a welder. Sparks rained down beneath the bright yellow car. Farther down the bay, a Porsche 911 sat with its hood open, another mechanic buried in the engine bay.

"You're staying busy."

Mike shrugged. "There's a track rally in Charlotte next month. Last-minute mods. We swapped out the gears on that 'Vette. Adding long tube headers now."

For a moment, the two men surveyed the graceful curves of the sport coupe, admiring every detail and precise crease of the bodywork. It was more than a car to them; it was art itself.

"Is it ready?" Reed asked.

Mike motioned to the back of the shop, and Reed followed him into another section of the building. Bright lights glared over a spotless double-bay garage with blue concrete floors and paint equipment lining the far walls. In the middle of the garage, Reed's 2015 Camaro Z/28 sat alone, its black tires gleaming. Bumper to bumper, the car was a deep, seductive red, with the Z/28 badges removed from the fenders and nothing left to identify it as the jet-black vehicle that ripped through Downtown Atlanta three weeks prior.

Reed ran his hand over the hood of his car. Even though the metal was as smooth and glossy as a brand-new Ferrari, he knew it wasn't painted. The car was still black but now sheathed in a high-performance synthetic wrap that perfectly conformed to the vehicle's every contour—a masterpiece in every way.

"I installed the supercharger and cranked it up to twelve pounds of boost," Mike said. "It's putting about six hundred eight horsepower to the wheels at full throttle. I also swapped the driveshaft with a carbon fiber replacement to sustain the added torque and switched out your lower control arms to help with traction issues. Oh, and I put wider wheels on the back. With that much power, you're gonna need all the rubber you can get."

Reed stuck both hands into his pockets, still staring at the car. "It's perfect."

Mike shoved a wad of chewing tobacco into his cheek. "You sure you don't wanna add some better pipes? With all that power, it could sound incredible."

Reed shook his head. "I'm not trying to make noise. Just speed. What about the transmission?"

"Tranny should be fine. It's well made. Just watch out for the brakes. They're too small for this much power. You really need bigger discs, but I didn't have time to replace them. You're gonna need some room to stop."

Reed nodded and retrieved a thick roll of hundred-dollar bills. Mike accepted it without counting and passed Reed the keys.

"You know . . . rumor has it a black Camaro made quite a lot of noise downtown a few weeks ago." A playful light danced in Mike's eyes.

Reed opened the driver's door. "Wouldn't know about that, Mike. My car's red."

The metal door of the garage rattled as Mike rolled it up. Reed twisted the key, and the engine rumbled to life, flooding the small space with the voice of freedom ready to be unleashed. He tapped the gas and listened to the subtle whine of the supercharger kick in, forcing air into the motor and churning out new levels of power.

Reed shifted into first and waved at Mike before rumbling out through the yard and onto the street. Somewhere out there, north of the city and in the mountains, there was a man they called The Wolf—a killer—an assassin's assassin. Two weeks prior, while Reed had been hunting Oliver Enfield amid those mountains, The Wolf had chased him twice in a silver Mercedes coupe with enough power to run down anything on the road.

Until now.

Reed scrolled through a short list of contacts on his phone. That list had grown shorter over the past few weeks as more and more of his former friends and colleagues faded into a grey area of untrustworthiness. Prior to Oliver Enfield's betrayal, Reed counted himself among an exclusive fraternity of elite killers, many of whom also worked for Enfield. Now, he couldn't be sure which of them might sell him out at the first opportunity. Reed was more limited than ever in who he could trust.

He hit the dial button and waited for the car's Bluetooth system to take over the call. The phone rang five times before a clattering sound rang over the speakers, then a nervous voice.

"Chris! Hey. Um, my phone was on the floor. Hold on a second."

More clattering. A dog barked in the background, and a child cried.

"Hey. Okay, I'm here now. Had to get my headphones."

"Is that a baby?" Reed snapped.

"What? Baby? Oh, no. That's the TV, man. Got my Netflix rolling in the background. You know what I'm saying?"

Reed rolled to a stop at a traffic light and ran his hand over his forehead. He tried not to sound as frustrated as he felt. "Dillan, I hired you to conduct research, not to watch Netflix."

"Oh, yeah, man. No worries. I work best with a little background noise."

"Okay . . . so do you have any results yet?"

"Results. Um, let's see here. . . ."

Each second that drained by grated on Reed's nerves as though it were a knife digging into his spine. "Dillan, have you found her or not?"

"Um, well, no. Not strictly speaking. But I'm pretty sure she's in the country!"

"What do you mean, you're *pretty sure?*"

"Oh, you're gonna like this. So you told me what bank she uses, right? I have this buddy who works there, and I got him to run a check on her account to see if there's any out-of-country spending. And there wasn't. Badass, right?"

Reed slammed his hand into the console of the car. "You involved a *third party?* Dillan, I told you this is highly confidential!"

"No worries, bro. My dude is totally discreet. He's also my weed dealer, so he knows how to keep things on the down-low."

"Did it ever occur to you that his computer use might be tracked? He might not be the only one who knows he checked into her accounts."

"He said it wasn't a problem. I'm not worried."

Of course you're not.

"Did you check to see where she *is* spending her money?"

"Yeah, well, I asked about that. Apparently, she took out a lot of cash in Atlanta, and nothing's happened since. But he's gonna check back in—"

"*No.* No, he's not. I don't want any more poking around at the bank. Banks are some of the most high-security, sensitive institutions in the world."

"Okay, how do you want me to find her, then?"

Reed spoke through gritted teeth. "*I don't know how.* That's why I hired a private investigator. Can you get it done or not?"

Dillan sighed. "Chill out, dude. I'll get it done. Just give me a few more days, okay? I'll holler at ya later."

The phone clicked off before Reed could add any further admonitions. He wrapped his fingers around the wheel and took a slow breath, forcing his tense muscles to calm. He didn't want to hire Dillan. It was anything but an ideal situation. In years past, he would've made a single phone call to the legendary sleuth of the criminal underworld known only as Winter, and within twenty-four hours, there would be an email in his inbox with his target's precise location. Winter was crazy good like that, but the genderless ghost wasn't accepting Reed's calls anymore and hadn't been since the events in North Carolina. That left Reed alone, blind, and without any hope of finding Banks Morccelli on his own.

He let his mind drift back to the last time he saw her, standing amid the trees next to the lake as rain washed over her pale face. Her eyes, so bright and beautiful, were strained with the pain and agony of betrayal as she stared down at the man she thought she loved. Reed stared back into the soul of the woman who held his heart in her hands, the only person he had left to hold. She didn't say a word as she turned into the trees, vanishing into the night and leaving him alone with the body of his former mentor lying at his feet.

In the two weeks since that night, Reed had searched all over Atlanta for Banks. It was only after days of fruitless searching that he hired Dillan, a local private investigator, to track her down. It was a desperate move, but he had to find her before anyone else did. The Wolf was still on the prowl, Oliver's shadowy employers were still at work in the dark, and Reed was likely the only person on Earth who could protect Banks from the war he had just started.

4

Special Agent Matthew Rollick of the FBI spent well over a decade as a homicide detective for the Los Angeles PD before making the career switch to federal investigation. During those long years, he'd seen everything from suicide by drowning to execution-style gang murder. Dozens of cases crossed his desk, and more than half of them were never solved. Blood, carnage, and the worst humanity had to offer were all par for the course during a normal day at the office.

But even after all of that, nothing could prepare him for the war zone beside the lake. By the time local law enforcement advised the FBI of a quintuple homicide outside of Lake Santeetlah, North Carolina, the bodies had long since been removed and the ashen remains of the cabin taped off, but the photographs were all there. Three males, all white, slaughtered by the river. The first was a bald man in his early sixties. A massive chunk of his lower back had been blown out by a shotgun, leaving dozens of tiny lead pellets embedded in his skin. His stomach, chest, and throat all sustained multiple knife wounds, and the left side of his face was missing, apparently also blown off by a shotgun.

Then there was the giant. A man of seven feet tall, no less than four hundred pounds, lay on the riverbank with the back of his head blown off by a shotgun. Two Georgia state policemen—state government guards, assigned to the cabin—lay farther up the bank, both with their throats cut.

And finally, stretched out in the mud, by himself, with a gunshot wound to his middle back, was Senator Mitchell Holiday. His face was the only one of the three still fully intact, leaving cold white skin and the lifeless eyes of a man who died in tremendous pain.

Agent Rollick stood next to the lake and closed his eyes, trying to visualize every angle of the crime scene as it must have looked when police first arrived. Shoe prints indicated four men, possibly five. A torrential downpour had begun close to the estimated time of death for all five victims, washing away most of the tracks and prints left in the mud, and leaving investigators to piece together the rest as best they could.

Four men. One of them with a shotgun.

Local police had indeed recovered a shotgun—an expensive twelve-gauge break-action weapon whose serial number was traced back to a purchase at a sporting goods retailer in North Georgia. A few hours of research produced a bill of sale from two years prior with Mitch Holiday's signature on it.

So the weapon belonged to Holiday, but it was difficult to believe that he used it. For one thing, there were at least two different sets of prints on the gun, and neither one of them matched the senator. And secondly, if he used the weapon, why was it found thirty feet away from his body?

Rollick walked back from the lake, gaining a vantage point over the crime scene where he could survey the whole area. It was a trick he learned back in LA—remove himself from the middle, gain a bird's eye view, and use his imagination to fill in the gaps.

Assuming there were four men in addition to the Georgia state policemen, that might explain why the shotgun was dumped thirty feet away from the bodies. It could also explain the multiple empty shotgun shells recovered farther up the hillside, near where the senator's two bodyguards were found dead. The fourth man was armed with a shotgun, directing gunshots toward everyone but the senator.

So was this guy protecting the senator? Holiday appeared to die from some manner of a large, heavy-caliber handgun or rifle fired close to his back. That explained the burned gunpowder residue that coated his shirt. Did the giant fire that weapon? If so, where was it?

"What do you think?" The voice came from behind, startling Rollick out of his muse. He turned to see Agent Liz Fido standing a few feet behind, a clipboard clamped between her petite hands. Fido had been his investigative partner for two weeks since his case involving Mitchell Holiday migrated from Atlanta and into the mountains of North Carolina, where Holiday was supposed to be under protective custody.

So much for that.

"I think we're screwed. Holiday was only weeks away from testifying. Now we'll never know what he had to say."

Fido twisted a toothpick between her lips. "You still think there was a fourth man?"

Rollick shrugged. "I don't see how there couldn't be. The fingerprints on the shotgun don't match any of the victims. I just don't get why all three men were so close to the lake while the cabin burned. Seems like they would've retreated to the parking lot."

"Holiday's Land Rover was pretty much totaled. Reports have it crashing through Cherokee County shortly before the estimated time of death. Maybe the fourth man used it, then returned, set fire to the cabin, and killed everybody down by the river."

"If that's the case, he must've been here before. The Land Rover was with Holiday when he arrived here. Unless this guy stole it, we can conclude this fourth man was a friend."

Fido plucked at her bottom lip with an index finger. "So then, maybe he didn't set fire to the cabin. Maybe it was already burning when he got back."

Rollick ran a hand over his face. His back ached, and he hadn't slept well in days—both compliments of the cheap hotel room the FBI rented him. "I don't know. We're working with too little information. The bottom line is we dragged our feet, and now our lead witness is dead."

Rollick started back toward the pile of ashes and charring timbers that remained of Holiday's lakeside cabin.

"What were you investigating him for anyway?"

Rollick kicked through the loose ashes of the burned-out home, toeing around for anything that survived the ravenous fire. "That's the weird thing. We got a tip about some smuggling operations down in Brunswick, and interviewed Holiday because we thought his logistics company might be inadvertently involved. He wasn't even a suspect at the time, but he flipped out. Got real jumpy, then eventually claimed he had proof of some kind of big conspiracy. But he wouldn't share anything without all these weird guarantees. I was stalling for time, hoping his nerves would get the better of him. He was clearly rattled."

Fido tossed the toothpick into the dirt. "Guess you stalled too long."

"I guess so. Look, we need to get the original DNA samples from local PD. I'm not satisfied with their analysis. I wanna run everything through DC."

"Have to get the new kid to do it. I'm being transferred to Charlotte."

"You're shitting me."

Fido shook her head. "Nope. New assignment of some kind. They're giving you a rookie fresh out of the Academy. Ex-Marine. I don't know much about him, but at least he's a blank slate. You can train him your way."

Rollick spat into the ashes and ground his heel over the mess. From day one, this entire investigation felt cursed. Bureaucracy, red tape, repeated partner changes, missing witnesses, and dead ends plagued his every move. Things looked up when Holiday was recovered from a trailer outside of Atlanta after his violent kidnapping from FBI custody, but everything fell apart when the senator still refused to testify. Everything about this case stank of organized crime—the kind of thing an FBI agent dreamed of investigating.

But no matter how hard he pushed, he hit nothing save block walls.

"Does this kid know *anything* about homicide investigation?" Rollick asked.

Fido shrugged. "Ask him yourself. That's him pulling up now."

Rollick peered through the trees as a Jeep Wrangler wound its way into the parking lot. The vehicle was old—at least twenty years—and red in color. Suspension groaned and exhaust gurgled as the Jeep rolled to a stop next to Rollick's agency-issued Impala, then the engine cut off.

"So long, Rollick. Good luck." Fido tossed him a two-finger salute, then walked toward her car.

Soft grey ashes spilled over Rollick's boots as he turned away from the parking lot and waded through the burned-out home. He knelt under what remained of the kitchen cabinets and sifted through the dirt and debris with his bare hands. A bent spoon, two glass beer bottles, and what appeared to be a double-A battery turned up, then Rollick's fingers collided with something hard and cold.

Boots crunched through the debris behind him. Rollick could feel the tense, all-business attitude of the rookie investigator spilling into the atmosphere. Damn, he hated ex-military agents. Sure, they were disciplined, hardworking, and universally respectful of the rules, but they lacked the outside-the-box imagination that, in his opinion, made for an ideal investigator.

"Agent Rollick?"

The man behind him spoke with a thick Southern accent. Rollick glanced over his shoulder, squinting through the sun at the broad-shouldered, thick-jawed man ten feet away. Yeah, he looked like a Marine.

"Get over here, kid. Help me with this." Rollick pried at the metal object, running his fingers around its smooth, round edge.

The big man knelt beside Rollick, and together they dug through fallen timbers, chunks of foundation, and sections of metal roofing. After a few minutes, the object became more visible amid the ashes. It was a large Dutch oven, turned upside down with the handles burned off. Rollick muttered a curse and kicked at it.

Another piece of shit.

The pot clicked against his foot, then rolled over, exposing a small rectangular object buried beneath. Kneeling back down, Rollick scooped it up and blew the ashes off.

Score.

It was a cell phone. The screen was busted, with chunks of glass missing and large cracks ripping through the remainder of the face. But the phone was still intact, and the best he could tell, untarnished by the flames.

Rollick handed the phone to his new partner. "Get this back to the lab. Have them run a full inventory of the memory. If they can recover the phone number, we'll subpoena the carrier to provide us a full list of the most recent calls and text messages."

The big man nodded. "I'm on it, sir."

Rollick turned toward his car. "I'm not your sir. I'm your partner. You can call me Rollick—or just Roll. If you want to thrive in the FBI, you work hard and keep your ear to the ground. Whatever you learned in the Marine Corps, you'll have to unlearn here. This isn't the military. This is an investigative agency. Our job is to find the bad guys, then supply enough evidence to the prosecutor to charge them. Then we're out. Understand?"

"Yeah. Got it."

Rollick stopped beside his car, dug out a stick of gum, then looked back. "You got a name?"

The big man offered his hand. "Rufus Turkman. Everybody calls me Turk."

Rollick grunted and accepted the handshake. "Welcome to the FBI, Turk."

5

The hotel room was small and dark, with peeling wallpaper and the kind of lumpy mattress that made you wonder what deformed dragon slept inside. That said nothing of the mold growing in the shower stall or the unidentifiable stains on the carpet. Baxter looked even less thrilled with the accommodations than Reed felt, but neither one of them commented as Reed closed the door and sat down on the bed.

"Baxter. Beer me."

The bulldog's wrinkled, scalded skin was a patchwork of singed hair and crimson. He peered up at Reed through beady black eyes and snorted, spraying snot and slobber over the floor.

Reed laughed and unzipped the suitcase. "I'm only kidding. Here. Time for your medicine."

Baxter dutifully climbed onto his dog bed, sitting silent and still as Reed massaged a medicated salve onto his wounds. When Reed's fingers traced the burn marks and swollen scars that crisscrossed his pet's back, Baxter cringed, but he didn't whine. He huddled against the bed until Reed was finished, then settled down.

"That's a good boy," Reed whispered. "You're getting better already."

The soft snores that rumbled from Baxter's open mouth weren't as smooth or peaceful as they used to be. There was pain in each labored breath, a hallmark of the trauma the dog had experienced two weeks before when he was caught in the midst of the house fire. Reed studied Baxter's slack lips, then scratched gently behind the bulldog's ears. In a lot of ways, Baxter was his only friend—his only companion during the long nights and bloody days that characterized his existence in Atlanta.

"We'll get them," Reed said. "We'll burn them the way they burned Kelly. I promise."

A thick binder at the bottom of the suitcase was bent and dirty, packed with folded papers, wrinkled photographs, and two or three pens. Reed spread the contents across the bed and sorted through each item until he located a small notebook. He pulled a pen cap off with his teeth and sat cross-legged on the bed with the notebook. A list of names lined the faded yellow paper, each scrawled in his own spidery handwriting. Oliver Enfield's name topped the list, with a thick red line scribed through it. The next name on the list was Cedric Muri. Reed scraped the pen across the name, obliterating it in an identical red line, then he tapped the third name. *Salvador.*

Reed didn't know his last name, but that didn't matter, because Salvador probably wasn't his real name anyway. A man in Salvador's line of work was certain to have multiple aliases. Whoever the unidentified South American truly was, he belonged on this list next to a kingpin killer and a mercenary broker. Salvador was the man most directly connected with the shadowy organization who wanted Mitchell Holiday murdered. He hired Cedric Muri to supply henchmen for Oliver's use in setting up Reed, and those same henchmen were responsible for kidnapping Banks and killing Kelly.

"Who are you, Salvador?"

Was he the head of the snake, or just another piece in a massive machine? Nothing about the events of the last month felt like the manipulations of a single man. If Reed knew anything about the criminal underworld, it was that nothing was ever as it seemed, and there was almost always another layer of puppet masters behind every fiendish action. Salvador was most likely just a boss, calling the shots on behalf of a bigger boss, and so on. The only way to know was to find him.

Reed stuck the list of names to the wall in front of the bed. One at a time, he taped each picture, note, and news article to the wall. Headlines documenting the events in Atlanta hung beside campaign photos of Mitch Holiday and charts outlining the structure of Oliver Enfield's criminal empire.

Reed stepped back and rubbed his chin, staring at the mess of data. He drew in a long sigh and turned to Baxter. "We're gonna be here a while, boy."

The dingy room was quiet, and though Baxter lay on the end of the bed with his eyes closed, Reed knew he wasn't sleeping. The old dog never slept without snoring, and now his breaths came in gentle wheezes between his teeth.

He's in so much pain.

Reed's eyes stung, and his head felt numb. He tipped the beer bottle and drained it, then tossed it on the floor next to half a dozen others. The carpet, a worn pattern of green with red flowers, blurred out of focus, and Reed didn't try to blink his way back into clarity. The flowers were dyed into the carpet's fibers, now flattened by years of dirty feet. He imagined he could see the bacteria and grime clinging to each twisted strand, crawling toward the beer bottles like an army of disease.

He embraced his headache and nausea. It was probably hunger, but he didn't have an appetite or any desire to leave the hotel room. A part of him wanted to stay there forever, lie back on the bed, let his mind drift into oblivion, and let them find him a week later.

Kelly. He saw her seductive smile as bright and dangerous as the first day he met her. He remembered that moment so clearly it almost felt real, as though it were happening all over again, here in his mind. Reed exhaled, savoring the memory. He could still feel the hot Mediterranean sun on his face, flushing his skin red as his heart pounded and sweat streamed from his face. The place was Monaco; the date was sometime in June of 2016. It was a memorable date because it was his first international contract. A casino drug lord crossed the wrong *hombre* back in Mexico City, and that *hombre* hired Oliver's company to settle his score. Oliver dispatched

Reed. It was Reed's sixth hit, and in a lot of ways, it was the trickiest. Reed decided to conduct the kill by strangulation, inside the drug lord's penthouse, high atop a downtown tower.

Everything went perfectly, right up until nothing did. There was a prostitute in the penthouse, and even though she was high as a kite on some narcotic, Reed knew she would remember everything. He had hesitated over the bed, staring down at the slain mob boss, then turned toward the prostitute with the choke wire still dangling between his fingers.

That moment of hesitation almost killed him. His original egress plan had been to take the service elevator to the bottom floor, hijack a car, and make his way to the coastal town of Cannes. Oliver would extract him via a charter boat two miles off the coast—a difficult but manageable swim. In the years that passed since that pivotal moment, Reed often wondered what would have happened if he hadn't spent those crucial twenty seconds standing over the prostitute, struggling to decide whether he should kill her. Maybe he could have dodged the security officers who came barreling through the penthouse door with their guns drawn. Maybe he wouldn't have been shot in the arm or forced to take the stairway, falling down the last two flights and breaking a rib in the process.

He escaped the guards, thanks to his rapid descent, but every breath was agony and his arm still bled. He ran from the lobby to the parking garage, his vision bloodshot and his head swimming, still clinging to his initial plan of hijacking a car.

And that's when it happened. He slammed into Kelly at the same moment she burst out of a service door and skidded toward a cherry-red Ferrari Spider 458. She wore a black sweatshirt with the hood pulled over her dark hair and a face mask covering her mouth and nose. When their eyes locked, a recognition of criminal kinship instantly registered in their eyes, and Kelly didn't hesitate.

After a quick manipulation of the ignition wires on the Ferrari, she jerked her head toward the passenger seat and slammed the car into gear. "Let's roll, kid. We're in this together now."

Reed piled into the car without question, ignoring the flashing red flags that erupted throughout his mind. Kelly stomped on the gas and piloted the vehicle out of the garage and onto the street. French police cars were already barreling toward them from all directions, but they didn't stand a chance. The shiny red supercar slid in and out of alleys, screeching around apartment buildings, and leaving the squad cars in a shower of golden Mediterranean sand.

Reed had never seen a woman drive like Kelly. With every twist of the wheel, her eyes shone as though she were a kid on a pony, working the paddle shifter with the grace and agility of a practiced master—a true racer.

Even now, Reed could still feel the wind whipping through the windows, tearing at their hair.

Ten minutes later he passed out from blood loss, remaining unconscious until he awoke in a hut buried deep within the French countryside. His wounds were stitched, his ribs braced, and Kelly sat beside him, watching the sunset over the gleaming outline of the supercar.

Her hood and mask were gone, exposing the sharp curves of defined features—a small mouth, a sharp nose, and high cheekbones. She wasn't beautiful in the traditional way, but at that moment, Reed had never seen a woman so gorgeous.

"That's not your car, is it?" he asked.

Kelly faced him with a broad, childish grin. "It is now."

Reed swallowed past a dry throat as the memory faded back into the foggy mist of the past. The months that followed with Kelly were a whirlwind of encounters around the world, carefully orchestrated to mesh with her car boosting and his assassination schedules. He never asked her about her curious career, and she never asked about his. From the start, they both knew it wasn't meant to last, but for an instant, he hoped it would.

He remembered Kelly's gentle words after the literal train wreck in Atlanta. *"I would have married you if you weren't such a walking disaster."*

She had left her successful career as a supercar thief after she found faith—some form of Christianity. He didn't understand it, and at the time, losing her to this strange, legal lifestyle ripped deeper than a simple breakup would have. Looking back now, he admired Kelly for making the jump that he only dreamed of—getting out, moving on, living a normal life.

And she almost made it.

Reed put his feet on the floor and fumbled with the phone. The tears that stung his eyes made it difficult to dial. He put the phone on speaker and cleared his throat.

"Lasquo Financial. How may I direct your call?" Lasquo Financial was a bank of sorts based out of New Orleans, specializing in managing the financial needs of the criminal underworld. As a contract killer, that included Reed. He read off his memorized series of coded passphrases, then requested to speak to Thomas Lancaster, his personal banker.

"One moment."

The hold music was gentle and soothing, but it couldn't fill the void that shredded through his soul. It only made it feel deeper and wider, every musical note echoing off the canyon walls in his heart and reminding him just how dark and empty he felt.

"Reed, my boy. Good to hear from you."

Reed cleared his throat. "Hey, Thomas. I wanted to check my investment balance."

"Let's see here . . ." Keyboard keys rattled. Thomas hummed a little. Reed ignored it all and thought about the French sunset falling behind the Ferrari.

"As of today you've got three-point-three million on investments. And change."

"That's perfect. Can you cash out a million for me?"

"Um, sure. May I ask why?"

"I lost somebody dear to me. I want to send some money to their parents."

"I'm so sorry to hear that, Reed. I can arrange it for you."

"Could you make it anonymous?"

The keyboard clicked again. "You know I can, Reed. What I usually recommend to my clients in this situation is to let me mail the money to the beneficiary as a life insurance check. I can set it all up through a shell company, and they'll be none the wiser."

"Perfect."

Thomas asked for names and addresses. Reed consulted his notebook and rattled them off, his mind still lost in a fog. Thomas read off a confirmation number but didn't hang up. Reed could hear the hesitation in his voice.

"Reed . . . there is another matter. Something happened a couple days ago."

"Yes?"

"A, um, gentleman came in inquiring about you. Small, South American fellow. Wanted to know about your recent spending, current location, etcetera."

The words rang in Reed's ears as facts with no emotional implication. What Thomas said should've concerned him, but he was too tired to be worried. "What did you tell him?"

Thomas snorted. "I told him what any self-respecting banker would tell a stranger inquiring about one of my clients. I invited him to have intercourse with himself."

Reed tried to smile. "Thanks, Thomas."

"I'm sorry I wasn't able to get his name."

"His name is Salvador, and I'm dealing with it. Thank you for letting me know."

Thomas coughed, his tone returning to its traditional, all-business formality. "Of course, Reed. Let us know if there's any way we can help."

Reed dropped the phone on the bed, then drew in a long, deep breath. He envisioned the flashing smile of the dark-skinned South American standing beside Oliver at Pratt-Pullman Yard, the first and last place Reed saw the man who called himself Salvador.

Regardless of whoever was behind this tangled mess of crime, deceit, and bloodshed, Salvador was to blame for what happened to Kelly. Her death, the death of her fiancé, and the death of her unborn baby were all on his hands. And Reed was going to roast him alive for it.

6

"Madam Governor! A moment of your time!"

"Madam Governor, can you comment on your administration's intentions concerning offshore drilling initiatives?"

"Madam Governor, has your cabinet reached any decisions with regard to a new attorney general?"

Maggie Trousdale stopped at the foot of the Capitol steps and turned to the crowd of reporters bustling in around her. The crush of bodies, the flash of cameras, and the clamor of voices overwhelmed her senses, igniting her trepidation about the office she had just been inaugurated into. When she first announced her candidacy for governor only fourteen months prior, she never imagined she would actually win. What business did a small-town girl from the Louisiana swamps have in running an entire state? She ran because she wanted to make a point—that corruption and bureaucracy had saturated her state for far too long, and that the new leader of Louisiana should be prepared to take on the challenges of Baton Rouge and the swamp of political mire it contained. She had no idea how strongly that message would resonate with the people of Louisiana, or how ferociously the citizens of Louisiana's rural towns would rally around the prospect of electing one of their own.

But it did, and they had, and now here she stood—a thirty-four-year-old governor of one of the most culturally and legally unique places in the country—overwhelmed beyond her mind.

The state troopers who stood at her elbows closed in and held out their hands, barking at the reporters. "Stand back! Stand back now!"

Maggie's shoulders slumped in exhaustion. It wasn't yet noon, but she had already put in an eight-hour workday. She couldn't remember her last shower, or whether she had eaten breakfast, but she wasn't going to ignore the reporters. They were the mouthpieces of the people, and the people were the reason she took this damnable job in the first place.

"First of all"—Maggie raised her hand, quieting the crowd—"I want to restate my extreme sorrow and sincerest condolences to the family of Attorney General Matthews. He was a good man, a loyal servant of Louisiana, and an outstanding prosecutor. My cabinet is shocked by his sudden passing and will be providing the Louisiana Bureau of Investigations every available assistance as they pursue an inquiry into his death. We—"

A reporter shouted over his colleagues' heads. "Does that mean you believe he was murdered, Governor?"

"I didn't say that." Maggie faced him directly. "At this time, I have been advised by Lieutenant Colonel Jackson of the LBI that there are no indicators of—"

"Yes, you said that yesterday. Shouldn't we know more by now?"

"As I stated already, we are not—"

A new reporter broke in. "Who will be his replacement?"

Maggie felt her cheeks flush, and she bit back the urge to curse. Enduring the constant interruptions and disregard for anything she was saying was an element of political pandering she was neither accustomed to nor predisposed to tolerate.

Instead of objecting, she decided to answer the question with a challenge of her own. "Ms. Simmons, isn't it?"

The reporter nodded, tapping a pen on her lip.

"Ms. Simmons, are you at all familiar with the Louisiana Constitution?"

The crowd was quiet now, and several of the reporters shot Simmons crooked smirks. She didn't answer, and Maggie cleared her throat.

"I thought not. If you were, you wouldn't have asked that question. Per our constitution, anytime the attorney general's office is unexpectedly vacated, the assistant attorney general assumes the office *unless* the remainder of the attorney general's term exceeds one year, in which case the governor calls a special election. Since Attorney General Matthews's term extends another twenty-two months, I will be announcing the scheduling of a special election for a replacement within the week. You can direct all further inquiries as to the identity of the new attorney general to the people of Louisiana."

Another outburst of questions blasted from the crowd. Maggie waved her hand and offered a tense smile. "That's all for today, everyone. Thank you so much."

She mounted the steps, turning back toward the Capitol. At four hundred fifty feet tall, Louisiana's Capitol building was the tallest in the nation, rising above the streets of downtown Baton Rouge in polished white marble. In Maggie's early days as a pre-law student at Louisiana State University, she often sat in the sprawling thirty acres of state gardens that surrounded the building and studied under its magnificent shadow. At the time, the building inspired her. It felt majestic, powerful, and secure. Now it only stressed her out—a pit full of political vipers, half of whom wanted to take her out as violently as possible.

Her shoes echoed on the marble floor as she crossed the main atrium and approached the elevator. Maggie never wore heels—she hated them with a passion. Most days, she wore simple brown hiking boots, only donning flat dress shoes when tradition absolutely commanded it. It was an odd choice for somebody who also had to wear dress clothes every day, but her supporters loved it. They called her Muddy Maggie, The Swamp Girl. One of their own.

As soon as the door smacked shut on her executive office, the voices began. Daniel Sharp, her lieutenant governor, rambled on about press releases and issues with the media. Yolanda Flint, her chief of staff, waved a handful of papers and entered meltdown mode over logistical problems for her visit to New Orleans the next day. Half a dozen aides talked at once, crowding around the board table and freaking out over ten different subjects Maggie didn't care about.

"Everyone!" Maggie clapped her hands, and the room fell suddenly silent. She rubbed her temples and pushed out the mental clutter of the press conference. This wasn't the time to join the mayhem. "I think it's time you all had a break. Take a twenty and get some fresh air."

Everyone exchanged tense looks, hesitating where they stood.

Maggie snapped her fingers. "That wasn't a suggestion, people. Let's roll."

The aides began shuffling toward the door, and Maggie redirected her attention to Dan and Yolanda. "Not you two. We've got a call to make."

The doors clapped shut behind the crowd of aides, and Maggie sat down at the head of the board table, pouring herself a tall glass of water and sucking down half of it while Yolanda launched into her spiel about logistics.

"Yolanda." Maggie tried not to snap. "I really don't care. Just make it happen."

"But what are you going to wear? I need to coordinate your appearance given the current nature of—"

"Yolanda. Did my predecessor have to coordinate his appearance every time he set foot outside the Capitol?"

"Um . . ." Yolanda twitched and clicked a pen in her hand.

"No, he didn't. And don't tell me it's because he was a man. We're not coordinating a dinner party, we're running a state. It doesn't matter what I wear. Now sit down, and chill out with the details."

Yolanda reluctantly settled into her seat, and Maggie finished the water. Dan sat next to her, interlacing his fingers and waiting for Maggie to speak. It was perhaps his most underrated talent—knowing when to shut the hell up.

Maggie punched the speaker button on the desk phone and waited for her secretary to pick up.

"Yes, ma'am?"

"Get me Lieutenant Colonel Jackson, please."

"One moment, ma'am."

Calm settled over the room, broken only by the occasional click of

Yolanda's pen. The twitch grated on Maggie's nerves, but she chose not to comment. There were bigger fish to fry.

"Madam Governor." Jackson's booming voice carried all the command and directness of a life spent serving the military and then the law enforcement needs of Louisiana. After twenty-three years in the National Guard, Jackson switched to the LBI and quickly rose in the ranks as one of the chief investigators of the Bureau, and then as their executive director. Maggie didn't know much about him, but she liked him. He never had time for bullshit.

"Lieutenant Colonel, thank you for taking my call. I have Lieutenant Governor Sharp and Chief of Staff Flint in the office with me. I wanted to see if you had an update on the Matthews investigation."

Jackson cleared his throat. Maggie could already detect his hesitancy.

"At this time, Madam Governor, my office is unable to provide a confident determination as to—"

"Lieutenant Colonel, I'm so sorry to interrupt you, but I'm not a politician. I'm a swamp-raised gator hunter. I will never hold your instincts against you, and I don't expect you to be infallible. All I expect is for you to be direct and honest with me at all times. Tell me what you *know*, and then tell me what you *think*."

Dead silence hung in the air. Dan raised both eyebrows, and Maggie shrugged—she had to try.

"Yes, ma'am. At this time, we know that Matthews was found dead at his lake house yesterday around six forty-five a.m. Initial impressions are that he died of heart failure. There are no apparent wounds on his body, and no one was present at the time of his death."

"Did he have any known heart conditions?"

"We're securing his medical records and running a full toxicology panel on his body. A complete autopsy could take as long as forty-eight hours."

"What are the initial impressions of his manner of death?"

"Like I said, we believe congestive heart failure—"

"You know what I'm asking, Lieutenant Colonel."

Jackson sighed. "Murder is a distinct possibility, Madam Governor. We found a broken whiskey decanter on the floor beside him. The contents were mostly evaporated, leaving us to believe he died no later than around three a.m. We're running tests on the residue, but initial results indicate the presence of toxic substances. We'll know more soon."

Maggie leaned back in her chair. "Very good. I want you to move your investigation in the direction of a homicide, then. If there's any chance Matthews was murdered, I don't want a second to be lost. Whatever resources you require will be made immediately available."

"Thank you, Madam Governor. If that is all, I'll get back to work."

"That's all. Thank you so much."

Maggie ended the call and turned to Dan. He cocked his head and pursed his lips but didn't say anything.

In typical fashion, Yolanda spoke first. "Madam Governor, I think it's imperative that—"

Maggie held up an index finger. "Hold that thought, Yolanda. I want to hear what Dan thinks first."

Dan took a sip of water, then set it down. "Well, there are only two options. Either he was murdered, or he wasn't. Jackson will find out soon enough. My initial impressions are that we need to be careful throwing around the M-word. If it was a natural or accidental death, we don't need the press storm that will come with accusations of homicide."

"I agree," Yolanda burst in.

Maggie knew the demon of rationale had possessed her to hire Yolanda, and though Yolanda was the most annoying person in the state, she was also the most organized and the best at managing staff.

"Why would someone murder an attorney general?" Maggie drummed her fingers on the desk.

Dan grunted. "I mean, I guess there could be a lot of reasons. It might be personal. Might be random."

"Not if it's poison. A gunshot to the chest with a shattered window and a missing jewelry collection is random. A kitchen knife to the gut is personal. But poison . . . that's premeditated. That's assassination."

Maggie relaxed back into her chair and enjoyed the silence that followed her comments. Her head pounded, but headaches were such a common part of her daily regimen that she hardly noticed.

Dan's words were soft but strong. "I think we should be extremely cautious with that line of thinking . . ."

Maggie sat up. "I know. But I want you to consider this. There might be a lot of reasons to murder an attorney general, but there's only one reason why you would *assassinate* him: because he was in your way. That means somebody out there is up to something that Matthews wasn't having any part of, and I'm not having any part of it, either. I want to hold a special election for a replacement as soon as possible."

Yolanda sat forward. "Madam Governor, I want to advise *extreme* caution with that proposal. Rushing into a special election doesn't provide people enough time to grieve, and it could be interpreted as an extremely insensitive action on your part."

"Yolanda, I'm not here to manage public perception. I'm here to lead this state. Without an attorney general we are left wide open to all manner of corruption. I will not leave the state crippled. Dan, assemble a proposal regarding the earliest possible date we can hold a special election and have that on my desk tomorrow. Thank you."

Without another word, Maggie walked out of the office and into the Capitol hallways. She breathed in a deep lungful of musty air and smiled at a couple state representatives. Never had she been so surrounded by people and felt so alone.

7

"Can I help you, sir?"

Reed laid the ID on the counter and spoke quickly, the way he imagined an impatient investigator spoke. "Chris Thomas, Georgia Bureau of Investigation. I'm here to have a look at Senator Holiday's residence."

The clerk behind the front desk gave the ID a glance, and then she shot Reed a wide smile. He was used to that smile. It was the one every nervous girl gave him when he played this impersonation game.

It's days like these I don't completely hate myself.

"Mr. Thomas, I'll just need to check with my manager."

"Agent." Reed forced himself to lean on the counter as he subtly replaced the fake state ID into his pocket and shot the clerk a wide grin. "It's Agent Thomas, actually."

The woman—she couldn't have been more than nineteen—blushed and nodded, then hurried off. Reed kept his head down and his fingers off the counter.

In the main lobby of the condominium tower were two security cameras in the back corners, and the best he could tell, as long as he kept his face down, they wouldn't record anything but the top of his head.

Seconds ticked into minutes, and Reed rubbed his fingers against his sleeve. He misread her, he thought. Maybe she wasn't as girlish and smitten as she at first seemed.

"Agent Thomas?"

Reed straightened and turned, still keeping his face ducked beneath the rim of the nondescript baseball hat he wore.

A chubby man with a goatee stood behind him, his chest puffed out and his shoulders thrown back with the air of somebody who wanted to look important and impressive but didn't feel that way. Reed had seen it many times before. You rarely had to convince somebody you were an agent, or an investigator, or somebody with governmental authority if you could *impress* them with the importance of your presence. Self-inflation took over at that point and drowned out the better judgment of your average American.

Reed shook the manager's hand and shot him a friendly but serious smile. At least he hoped that's what it looked like.

"Don Burk," the chubby guy said. "Assistant manager and activities director at this property. Elizabeth tells me you were inquiring about Senator Holiday's residence. May I see your ID?"

Reed passed him the card. "That's right, Director."

Don's cheeks flushed at the word *director*. He made a show of examining the card, but Reed could tell he had no actual idea what a GBI ID should look like.

"I'd love to help you," Don said. "It's always my pleasure to cooperate with law enforcement. Unfortunately, I cannot allow entrance into a resident's unit without a warrant. I'm sure you understand."

Reed nodded. "Of course. My office faxed you the warrant this morning."

Don frowned, then shot Elizabeth a semi-accusatory glare. She shook her head once, then turned to check the printer.

"I'm afraid we didn't receive that fax, Agent," Don said. "Are you sure they had the number right?"

Reed made a show of running his hand over his face and sighing. "I'm sorry. It's been a hell of a week. You'd think something as important as the *assassination* of one of our own senators would garner a little more support from downtown. Nothing but yahoos down there."

Don's shoulders slumped a little, and Reed patted him on the arm with an understanding smile. "Don't worry, Don. I know you'd help me if you had the power."

Reed turned away.

And three, two . . .

"Wait!" Don snapped his fingers, then motioned Reed toward the hallway. "Step this way, Agent."

Reed followed the chubby manager into the hallway.

Don spoke in a conspiratorial whisper, his cheeks jiggling with every step of his stubby feet. "Strictly speaking, this is against corporate policy. But as the manager on-site, of course I have the power to make emergency exceptions in the name of public security. Can that be our little secret?"

Reed winked and patted Don on the back. "You got it, Director. Can't say how much I appreciate this."

"No problem. Anything for the GBI. Just get me a copy of that warrant, ASAP."

Don led the way into the elevator and mashed the button for the fourteenth floor. Reed crossed his arms and waited as the elevator groaned and began to rise.

Don wiped the sweat from his forehead and adjusted his vest in the way only a self-conscious man would. "You know . . . I knew the senator. Used to say hello every time he came in."

"Is that right?"

"Oh yes. Senator Holiday and I were on a first-name basis. I was pretty messed up when he passed. Seemed like a good man."

"He was." As the words escaped his lips, Reed wondered if they were true. He thought back to the cabin and Holiday's words on the front porch while they shared cigars. How broken the senator sounded, speaking of his mistakes. Maybe Holiday wasn't a good man at all. Maybe he was conflicted and war-torn. Certainly, there were redeemable things about him. He treated Banks well, at least.

The elevator ground to a halt and the doors rolled back. The hallway that stretched out ahead of them was pretty much what Reed expected for a building of this class—smooth hardwood floors with clean walls painted in a soft cream. Gold knobs and locks adorned every door, with golden light fixtures mounted overhead. It smelled clean, too.

Reed followed Don down the hallway and around a corner to a doorway mounted in the far wall. The numbers "1409" hung on the door—also in gold. Don fished a key from his pocket and pressed it into the lock. The door opened without a sound, exposing a dark room on the other side.

"Here you are. Senator Holiday's residence."

Don made no move to leave, and Reed smiled at him. "Thank you so much. If I could have the room, please."

The chubby manager nodded and cleared his throat. "Of course. Let me know when you're finished."

He disappeared back toward the elevator, and Reed stepped inside the condominium. He pushed the door shut with the toe of his boot, then tugged a pair of surgical gloves from his pocket. They snapped around his wrists as he pulled them on, sucking tight against his big hands.

The metal switch on the wall snapped with surprising aggression as Reed flipped it on, flooding the kitchen with white light. A thin layer of dust already clung to the surface of the counters and appliances, but nothing was left out of place. The room was orderly, right down to the neat row of coffee mugs next to the sink.

Reed moved into the adjoining living room. Through the floor-to-ceiling windows, he looked out over the Millennium Gate Museum, the duck pond that sat beside it, and the park beyond that. In the far distance, over seven hundred yards away, the outline of Ikea sat amid the low hills and thick trees of North Atlanta. Reed remembered lying on top of that Ikea only a month prior, staring through the scope of a high-powered rifle as he aligned the crosshairs with this very living room. He remembered watching Holiday laugh and talk on his cell phone as he walked back and forth across the room, drinking wine. The senator looked relaxed as Banks walked through the door.

Banks.

Reed closed his eyes and again saw her walk into the kitchen through the magnification of his rifle scope. He saw her embrace her godfather and accept a glass of wine. That was the moment his whole universe turned upside down—the moment worlds collided, and he made the decision not to press the trigger.

I had no clue what I was stepping into.

No, he hadn't known. He had no way of knowing. But even now, in the middle of it all, the reality of his decision paradigm hadn't changed a bit.

I'd do it again.

Reed turned away from the window and stepped back into the kitchen. A quick search of the cabinets revealed nothing but a sparse collection of dishes and a few canned goods. Past the bare living room, a single door blocked off the bedroom. Reed tried the knob and found it locked.

Who locks their bedroom when they leave?

A quick manipulation of the keyhole with his lock pick produced a satisfying click, and the door opened. If the living room and kitchen were sparse and clean, the bedroom that opened beyond the door was anything but. Mounds of dirty laundry, books, newspapers, and every manner of trivial trash were heaped against every wall, barely leaving room for the twin-size bed in the middle. The reek of unwashed clothes, stale food, and God knew what else filled his nostrils.

Reed took a step back and held his hand over his nose. As his eyes adjusted to the dimmer light of the room, he surveyed the mountains of trash. In one corner, a stack of six file boxes leaned to one side with sheaves of paper falling out. Bold black letters were written on the boxes, labeling them as case files from Georgia's third state senate district. The piles of newspapers were wadded up beneath stacks of old, dusty books—everything from murder mystery novels to medical research textbooks. Reed retrieved his flashlight and clicked it on. The pale pool of light spilling over the room illuminated more dust and dirt. Reed sighed and began to sift through the books.

"What happened, Senator? Who broke you?"

He thought about the carefully manicured and poised individual he confronted at the cabin in North Carolina. Even the slobbering, terrified version of Mitch Holiday that he kidnapped in Atlanta was more collected and mentally refined than the bedroom indicated. Senator Holiday was a man of deep and dark secrets, and Reed wondered if his mental state was less stable than it appeared.

Also piled with books and case files was a nightstand next to the bed, from which a small brown notebook stuck out. Reed pried it free and sat down on the bed, flipping open the worn leather cover. Dust ballooned into the air as he flipped the crinkled, water-damaged pages. Most were empty, but as he thumbed toward the back of the book, a short scrawling of black ink in strained handwriting filled the pages.

September 3

Agents from the FBI have contacted me regarding the investigation. I'm working with a man named Matt Rollick. I don't know what he knows. I'm afraid to talk to him. I'm afraid of what will happen to Banks, or what they'll say about Frank. I didn't mean for any of this to happen—I just wanted to make things better. I won't talk to the FBI. I won't do a damn thing until they can promise Banks will be protected. I'll take my secrets to the grave if I have to. Oh, God . . . I'm so sorry. I'm so sorry. I'm so sorry.

Reed flipped the page, exposing a crude drawing of a farmhouse in the mountains, surrounded by apple trees. The next several pages were sketches of farms, empty roads, and valleys between the mountains. Reed flipped through the notebook, searching for more diary entries. He stopped over an entirely black page colored in with a pen. He froze over the drawing, maneuvering the flashlight until it illuminated the whole page. A black hole was surrounded by more darkness. In the middle of the hole, wreathed in shadows, was the face of a devil, with sharp, glaring eyes, horns, and vicious fangs. At the bottom of the page, written in shaky letters, were two words: *He knows.*

Reed's blood turned to ice as the demonic face watched him, judged him. He slapped the journal shut and dropped it clumsily on the nightstand, his hands suddenly sticky and numb. The notebook slipped off the table, and as it hit the floor, a dull *clunk* echoed from beneath the bed. Reed dropped to his knees and ran his hand beneath the bed skirt. His fingers collided with something hard and metallic, and he dragged it out, exposing a small black box with a key lock.

Dust hung in the air as Reed settled on the floor and pulled out his lock pick again. His chest was tight with tension, and sweat dripped off his nose.

The lock stuck and resisted his attempts to defeat it. He continued twisting and manipulating the tool, working the tiny keyhole until he felt the latch click.

The lid fell to the floor in a poof of dust, exposing a single blank white envelope. Reed tore it open and shook it until a wallet-size photograph spilled out into his hands. It was printed in color but was worn and faded, as though it had spent the majority of its life in an actual wallet or on the dash of somebody's car.

There were only two people in the photo. Right away, he recognized the young man on the left by his thick hair and bold features. It was Holiday. A much younger, thinner Holiday, for sure, but definitely him. The second person in the photo was also young, but a little older than Holiday. He had sandy yellow hair and piercing blue eyes—eyes Reed would've recognized anywhere. They were the same as Banks's. This had to be Frank Morccelli, her father.

Both Holiday and Morccelli were dressed in black robes, and neither one of them smiled, with expressions bridging beyond serious to grim. The backdrop behind them was a black wall with the face of an owl etched in silver between their heads. Its eyes were painted red and glared out over their shoulders.

What the hell?

On the back of the photograph, written in Holiday's now-familiar scrawl, were two short lines: *Vanderbilt University, 1989. ΩΑΩ.*

Reed leaned against the bed and tapped the photo against his knee. He wasn't surprised by the Vanderbilt note—Winter had told him Holiday attended Vanderbilt University, which was where he met and became close friends with Frank Morccelli during the late eighties. He also remembered Winter mentioning that Holiday shared a fraternity with Morccelli, which would explain the Greek letters. What letters were they, anyway?

Reed tried to recall any residual knowledge he had about the Greek alphabet, though there wasn't much—he knew there was an Alpha and a Beta. He had encountered the Greek alphabet a couple times in church. David and Tabitha Montgomery were big on church when Reed was a child, and once or twice the pastor taught on the Book of Revelation, discussing the end-times. There was something about the Greek alphabet buried amongst those confusing prophesies, wasn't there?

Yes. He remembered now. It was something God himself said: *"I am the Alpha and the Omega, the beginning and the end."*

Reed sat up. He held the photo into the light that spilled through the blinds. The Greek letters on the back of the photograph were *"Alpha"* and *"Omega,"* the first and last letters of the Greek alphabet. Only they weren't written in that order; they were written the other way: last, first, last.

Holiday's final words echoed in Reed's head. He remembered kneeling beside the lake with the dying senator in his arms. He remembered leaning in and making out Holiday's final, whispered words. *"From end to end."*

From Omega to Omega.

Reed kicked trash away from his feet and hurried toward the door, pocketing the photo. Whatever dark, terrible secret lay behind the tragic life of Mitchell Holiday, it began at Vanderbilt University in 1989. It began with Omega Alpha Omega.

8

Salvador knew what death smelled like. Not the actual decaying part, where the body rots and the flesh falls away from the bone, but what *impending* death smelled like—that distinct, burning odor of something about to go terribly wrong. The stench of the grim reaper's rotting cloak as he stepped toward his next victim. After years of work on the dark side of the law, Salvador could smell the grim reaper a mile away, and today, the guardian of the grave smelled a lot closer than that.

"Give me your weapons."

At the front door of the lonely brick home, standing by itself on the outskirts of the city, Salvador shuffled from one foot to the other. His body ached from the sleepless nights and constant strain of the previous few weeks. He was used to it. He didn't mind the sleeplessness or the pressure, but he only appreciated the smell of death when he was the one bringing it. Feeling detached and out of control was perhaps the most terrifying reality he could imagine.

The cold European blocking his way was neither tall nor broad but still carried the savage air of a man who could squeeze the life out of Salvador with one hand. There was nothing but cold death in his eyes—no love, no warmth, no joy. This man was a killer.

Salvador unholstered his Italian-made Beretta .40 caliber pistol and handed it to the guard. The steel gaze didn't break contact with his own, and Salvador reluctantly pried the knife out of his belt and handed it over, also. The guard grunted then stepped to one side. Salvador sucked in a deep breath, forced himself to relax, and pushed the door open.

It was still midday, but inside the mansion was as dark and empty as the grave itself. Thick curtains hung over the windows, blocking out all light, and none of the fixtures mounted into the walls and the ceiling were illuminated. The rooms were bare—no furniture, decorations, or artwork. The home felt abandoned, as though it were going under foreclosure.

Another guard appeared out of the shadows and motioned Salvador onward. Their footfalls echoed through the whole house as Salvador followed him down a hallway, through two more doors, and finally into a sunroom on the backside of the house—or at least it was *supposed* to be a sunroom. The windows were painted black, and every corner was buried in shadows.

Salvador stopped just inside the room and turned toward the guard. The man was gone as quickly and suddenly as he'd appeared, vanished back into the shadows, and leaving Salvador alone in the shaded confines of the sunroom. He turned back toward the wall of glass panels and took a step farther into the shadows.

"That's far enough." The voice came from the far end of the room.

Salvador stopped and leaned forward, squinting into the darkness. "I can't see you."

"You're not supposed to see me."

A chill ran down Salvador's spine, and his feet were rooted to the floor. He listened for the breathing of another human being or the creaking of the floor beneath a footfall, but there was nothing.

"Gambit?" Salvador asked, his voice tentative.

"It was a simple request, wasn't it?" The voice rustled like wind over dry leaves. Empty. Unfriendly. Salvador recognized that voice—it was the voice of the man who hired him to assassinate Mitchell Holiday. The voice of the shadowy apparition known only as *Gambit*. But before, when Salvador accepted the job and was paid, Gambit's tone was warm and calm. Almost friendly. Now each word sounded as though it were being dragged over jagged ice.

"What request?" Salvador played for time.

"*Killing Mitchell Holiday.*"

The knot in Salvador's stomach twisted, sending panic through his mind. He sucked in a breath and shoved his hands into his pockets to keep them from shaking.

"Yeah, well, I took care of it. I hired the best."

"You hired *Oliver Enfield*, and he made the crucial error of putting his own interests ahead of ours. Apparently he was more interested in framing one of his own contractors than he was in completing the job."

Salvador nodded. "Yeah, that's how he operates. When one of his contractors becomes a problem, he sets them up. Lets them take the fall for the kill, so it's a clean slate."

"Did I *ask* for a clean slate?" Gambit's voice rose into a shout, and the windowpanes rattled in their frames.

Salvador swallowed hard. "You—"

"*I didn't.* I asked for a kill, plain and simple. You left me with a dumpster fire and a rampaging assassin!"

"You mean Montgomery? Look, I can take care of that. I've got another guy who supplies me the men I need—"

"*Cedric Muri?*"

Salvador hesitated.

"Muri's dead. Montgomery killed him two nights ago in his own casino. We have the whole thing on the security camera. You see, Salvador, when I hired you, I was under the impression that you were the man to get the job done. But it seems you're incapable of doing anything on your own. In fact, your entire methodology appears to be that of a cheap middleman—brokering out the dirty work to one subcontractor after another."

The panic rising in Salvador's chest began to take over. He took another step back and held up his hands. "Look, I operate with subcontractors for a reason. It gives you multiple layers of insulation from the kill. You know what I mean? I underestimated Montgomery, I admit it. But it's okay. I've still got assets in the field. Have you heard of The Wolf? He's not one of Enfield's men. He's an independent. A freelancer!"

"The same freelancer who let Montgomery off the hook in North Carolina?"

"Right, I know. That was my mistake. Oliver wanted to handle it himself, so I called The Wolf off. But Holiday bit the dirt, right? The job got done."

"After *two weeks*."

Salvador tried to step back again, but his foot hit the wall. "Listen. I screwed some stuff up, but I've got it. Give me a couple more days. The Wolf can get the job done—he just needs the right motivation. He's got this sister with cystic fibrosis in New York. It's leverage, right?"

Silence answered his sales pitch. The room around him was all at once darker and more closed in, as though even the walls bent their ill will upon him. He wanted to start again, renewing his arguments and mixing in additional excuses, but his better judgment finally took over. Any excuses now would be met with cynicism and perhaps vengeance.

"My boss is a patient man," Gambit said at last. "I'm not. You have three days."

A rustle of footsteps echoed from the far end of the room, and the speaker was gone—a shadow fading into deeper shadows.

Salvador sucked in a breath, then gritted his teeth. His patience with The Wolf's quirky behavior was about to cost him his life. It was time to take off the gloves.

9

"Chris! I found her." Dillan's words fell over one another in an excited stream. "She's in Nashville."

Reed held the phone away from his ear, wincing at the shrill noise. "I know."

He could almost hear the air whistling out of Dillan's deflating chest. "You . . . know? How? It took me two weeks!"

"Basic deduction. Don't worry about it. I'll send your payment."

"But—"

Reed hung up and downshifted the Camaro into third. The massive motor bellowed, and the supercharger screamed to life, blasting air into the engine block and pumping out additional horsepower. The back wheels of the car gripped the pavement and slung the Camaro forward. Vehicles flashed by on all sides as Reed navigated onto the freeway and swerved past a semitruck. Baxter lay in the passenger's seat, his tongue lolling out of the side of his mouth, dripping drool onto the floor mat. For the first time since the fire, his eyes weren't completely dominated by pain.

After returning from Holiday's condo, Reed stripped the hotel of any identifiable material and packed his gear into the trunk of the Camaro, then loaded Baxter into the passenger's seat. The smart thing would have been to leave him at a local animal boarder, but Reed didn't have the heart to abandon the dog again. For better or worse, Baxter would accompany him on the four-hour drive through North Georgia and into Tennessee.

The realization of where Banks fled to after the slaughter in North Carolina hit him only moments after uncovering the secret of Holiday's association with Banks's father, Frank Morccelli. Vanderbilt University was nestled in Midtown, Nashville. "Music City" had grown explosively over the past decade, expanding into a thriving tourist town packed with live-music bars and college kids. Reed recalled Banks's decision to leave Mississippi after her father died and take shelter with her godfather in Atlanta. Now that he too was gone, Banks would take refuge in the next most familiar place—Nashville, the town of her father's alma mater, and a place she frequently visited as a child. She wouldn't go home to face her vindictive mother, and she wouldn't disappear into a strange and lonely new place.

Reed was grateful that Banks was in Nashville because he didn't want to have to choose between pursuing his investigation and finding her. As soon as he reached the city, he would find a place to set up camp and give Baxter a bed, then look for Banks. There would be time to investigate Holiday's fraternity ties and make progress on finding Salvador afterward.

The sun began its western descent as the big car purred over the Georgia mountains and descended toward Chattanooga. The old town sat on the state line between Georgia and Tennessee, in the bottom of a valley and wrapped on three sides by the Tennessee River. Reed had driven through it many times before and always appreciated the charm of the dusty brick buildings and slow, methodical, Southern lifestyle. In a lot of ways, Chattanooga was stuck in another time—a calmer time.

As the exit signs flashed by on his right, Reed made the impulse decision to turn off the highway. Exhaustion burrowed deep in his bones, and his eyelids were already growing heavy. After two days of sleeplessness and who knew how much alcohol, it was past time to get some rest. He would stop here for the night, get dinner, then arrive in Nashville well before lunch the next day. It would be better not to confront Banks exhausted.

In typical fashion, as soon as Reed located a pet-friendly motel and reapplied Baxter's salve for the evening, his sleepiness vanished, and insomnia returned. He lay on the bed, staring at the ceiling for half an hour before he pulled his boots back on and stomped down to the front desk. A dirty desk clerk with a stained shirt and greasy hair watched him through smudged glasses, his gaze hazed over by some type of narcotic.

"What do you do for fun around here?" Reed asked. It was a poor choice of words.

"I dunno, man. Get high, I guess. You want some weed?"

"No, I mean I want to stretch my legs. Is there any place to . . . hike or something?"

"Oh, yeah, man. This is Tennessee. Lots of hiking, man."

Reed waited. The clerk stared at him with a blank expression, as though Reed weren't even there.

Reed rapped his knuckles on the counter. "So, where do I go?"

"Oh, yeah. Sure. Sunset Rock, man. It's really nice this time of the day. I go up there and get high all the time."

"Thanks."

Reed piloted out of the city, turning down one winding road after another as he followed his GPS into the mountains. Naked trees clung to the sides of rock cliffs, their ghostly limbs trailing over the pavement. With each switchback and curve, Reed drove farther above the valley floor. Many of the signs he passed advertised a place called Ruby Falls, while others mentioned Lookout Mountain. He was vaguely familiar with both locations, but he'd never been before.

After twenty minutes of weaving through small neighborhoods, the GPS led him to a tiny parking lot directly adjacent to the road. He squeezed the Camaro between two SUVs and climbed out, enjoying the blast of chilly mountain air. It was thinner and fresher than the smog-laden humidity of Atlanta, and after only a moment, it bit through his shirt and sent a shiver down his spine. Reed pulled a jacket out of the trunk and slid it on.

A trail led from the parking lot and into the trees, paved in thick slabs of rock that were half-path, half-steps, winding down the mountainside. Reed's muscles ached with every footfall, refreshing the agony of a dozen minor wounds that covered his body. Matched with bruises and stitches, his skin looked like the patchwork of Frankenstein's monster. The last month hadn't been kind to him, but even so, the exercise felt great. It revived his tired mind and brought clarity to his thoughts.

After less than a quarter mile, the trees parted all at once, exposing a wide rock ledge that jutted out from the cliff face and hung over the valley. Air rushed from Reed's lungs as he stepped off the trail and admired the rolling valleys of East Tennessee stretched out in front of him as far as he could see—miles of perfectly clear landscape cresting into mountain ranges on every side. The freeway wound through the valley floor a couple thousand yards away, each passing car and truck cruising across the valley floor at highway speeds, but at this distance, appearing to move at little more than a crawl. To his right, the western edge of Chattanooga was barely visible around the curvature of a mountain ridge, tall buildings reflecting the sunlight as the wide Tennessee River wound its way alongside the freeway. It was the most picturesque, gorgeous view Reed had ever scene—perfect and calm.

He took another step closer to the edge and felt his stomach churn. From this angle, he knew he was a few hundred feet high—enough to send his mind spinning and his every instinct commanding him to return to the car. But the view was too calming and beautiful. Reed forced himself forward another few yards, then sat down on a rock with his feet inches from the cliff's edge. He released a deep breath, liberating his tension and fear to the valley floor below and allowing a deep relaxation to settle in its place. The soothing touch of the sun on his face and the wind in his hair loosened his taut nerves, bringing gradual relaxation to his body.

Nearby, a young couple next to the cliff were wrapped in each other's arms. Farther on, a photographer with a camera and tripod attempted to replicate the stunning view. It wouldn't be easy. Something about the magnificent experience of sitting this close to the edge, saturated in the kiss of the sunset, was too raw and real to be appreciated by a photograph.

Reed closed his eyes and savored the bite of the wind. It was too cold to be comfortable, but the chill reminded him of the snow falling around his face as he and Banks crashed through the North Carolina mountains, desperately searching for a place to take shelter. At the time, all he felt was panic and a dreadful sensation of failure, but those feelings quickly melted into passion and warmth as he stood in front of a crackling fire and embraced Banks. He remembered the touch of her skin, the elegance of her kiss. It was the most perfect, beautiful feeling, too overwhelming and gripping to resist.

He opened his eyes and squinted into the sun. There was something about Banks—something profound that felt more solid than the mountaintop under his feet. It was something he never found in the Los Angeles gangs, the Marine Corps, or in Kelly's arms. All of those places offered him thrills and belonging and the promise of fame and fortune, but with Banks, it was deeper. It was a place to let his guard down and *be*, as though she had no expectations of who he was or what he could do for her—only what he could *be* for her.

The thought ripped through his heart like a bullet. Banks never cared about his real name, his occupation, his paycheck, or the chaos that accompanied their every encounter. She only cared about who he was and the way he made her feel. Maybe he made her feel safe, too. Maybe he felt like home to her in the way she felt like home to him. It was such a simple, beautiful thing, and he shattered it right in front of her face.

Reed retraced his memories back to that moment on the bank of the lake with Oliver Enfield dying at his feet. Mitchell Holiday, only a few yards away, was also gasping on his last breaths. The rain beat down from overhead as Banks stared at him, heartbroken, her tears mixing with rain as she dropped the shotgun and turned away.

I failed her. I crushed all the trust and faith she ever gave me.

Reed stood up, swallowing back the fear that overwhelmed his body, then took a step toward the edge, his hands held at his sides, fingers clenched.

She believed in me, and I proved her wrong. I've never been good. I've never been a home for anyone.

The valley floor opened up beneath him as his toes approached the edge. He could see hundreds of feet down the cliff face, into the belly of the gorge.

What am I fighting for? Oliver is dead. Who cares whether Salvador isn't? I don't deserve to be alive.

The wind beat at his shirt, plastering it back over his torn and marred chest. His feet were glued to the stone, as though he were no longer in control of his legs. He focused on each muscle group, commanding them one at a time. Lifting his toes, he inched his foot forward until it overhung the cliff. He stared down to the rocks below and imagined the next step: leaning forward, opening his hands, and letting go of his will to live.

So close.

He saw Kelly's sharp features and imagined her in the fire, slowly burning alive as her home caved in around her. He pictured her that first day in Monaco, her face obscured by the mask as she broke into the Ferrari. He heard her sassy, snapping voice again. *"Let's roll, kid. We're in this together now."*

"Hey, man. You okay?"

The voice ripped through his mind, shattering the memory. His eyes snapped open, and he turned to his left. The photographer stood a few feet away, his face twisted into a concerned frown. Farther down the cliff, the young couple, still in each other's arms, stared in semi-panic.

Reed stepped away from the ridge, shoved his hands into his pockets, and brushed past the photographer. "I'm fine."

The mountain steps strained his legs as he fought his way back up the trail to the parking lot. By the time he slid into the Camaro, his breath came in short gasps, and sweat dripped from his forehead. He wasn't out of shape, but he ached from the perpetual abuse of the past month.

He set his hands on the wheel and returned to that memory, there in the cottage in the middle of rural France. *"We're in this together."*

Kelly didn't abandon him when he stood in that French garage, dripping blood, and chased by an army of cops. She didn't abandon him beside the train tracks in Atlanta when he lay with an unconscious Banks in his arms, only moments from impending death. She didn't even leave him when he intruded on her perfect suburban life and asked her to watch Baxter—a favor that cost her life. She never let him down, never cut him loose, even when she should have. He wouldn't let her down now. He would wage war until her death was avenged and her enemies joined her in the ashes.

Then, and only then, he would die.

10

Reed had never been to Chattanooga's riverfront before, but there was something altogether familiar and calming about the gentle breeze that churned off the dark water and whistled over the dockside. The Tennessee river wound in graceful curves through the heart of the old city on its long journey south, leaving ample room for riverfront next to a downtown park. A large paddle cruiser rested at anchor with the name *Southern Belle* scrolled over the front in decorative letters. Just next to the boat, a metal, grated pier shot out over the river.

The sun had long ago set over the mountains, leaving Chattanooga dark and quiet as cars faded from the streets, and the business district fell asleep. After spending a few hours sitting in the hotel room staring at his feet, Reed decided to venture down to the water's edge before popping a sleeping pill. He resented the idea of taking any drug that would alter his state of mind, but it was now close to midnight, and he felt too exhausted and too frustrated with insomnia to argue. Maybe the fresh air would help.

The pier's metal grate squeaked beneath him. The river water lapped gently against the pilings, reminding him of the days when his father would load up the family in his old 1969 Camaro, and the three of them would drive five hours to the beach for the weekend. The waves lapped against the piers in Panama City much the same way, but the air didn't smell of fish and oil. It smelled of salt and sun and all things summer.

At the end of the pier, five flag poles stood bolted to the railing, with American flags snapping in the wind at the top of each. As Reed approached, he made out the shape of small, steel plaques fixed to the railings next to each pole, and recognized the familiar outline of the Marine Corps symbol engraved at the top of the nearest plaque.

He clicked on his flashlight. A simple memorandum was etched into the steel next to the Eagle, Globe, and Anchor:

LET US NEVER FORGET . . . THIS IS DEDICATED TO THE MEMORY OF LCPL WELLS, WHO PROUDLY SERVED, PROTECTED OUR COUNTRY, AND GAVE HIS LIFE TO OUR COMMUNITY ON JULY 16, 2015.

A weight descended over Reed's chest, and he stepped back from the plaque. He bowed his head, breathing in the musty air of the river.

I should've died. None of this would've ever happened if I had fallen, and Lance Corporal Wells had come home. He deserved to come home.

Reed swallowed back the guilt and straightened his back, then lifted his hand to his brow in a stiff salute toward the flags. The Stars and Stripes flipped in the wind, hanging as eternal guardians of the fallen. Somehow, he didn't feel worthy of saluting that flag. He didn't feel worthy of standing next to the plaques and remembering the fallen. Yet, at the same time, he couldn't walk away without the salute.

"Wow. You're still a patriot."

Reed recognized the sharp tone and inflection instantly, and even before he turned around, he was already reaching for the revolver strapped under his coat.

The man they called *The Wolf* stood only inches behind him, his lips lifted into a grin as his fingers twirled around a long, plastic-coated choke wire. Before Reed could wrap his hand around the grip of the weapon, The Wolf stepped forward and flicked the wire with an expert twitch of his fingers. It glided through the air and encircled Reed's head, cutting into the back of his neck and pulling him off-balance in an instant. He fell forward with a grunt and clattered onto the grating, struggling to roll over as The Wolf landed on his back. An iron kneecap crashed down between Reed's shoulder blades just as the wire slid beneath his chin and then tightened around his windpipe.

It all happened in mere seconds. Reed's world blurred as the grating cut into his chest. He choked and flailed with both arms, but the wire cut deeper into his neck, sealing off his throat.

"Seriously." The Wolf spoke without a hint of exertion in his tone. "If I'd been through half the crap you've endured, I'd hate this country."

Reed kicked out with both legs, twisting and wriggling from beneath the weight bearing down on his back, but he couldn't break free or reach his attacker. The deadlock was perfect—enough to keep him planted on his chest while his thundering heart consumed what precious oxygen remained in his lungs.

"All right, my dude. You have to die now. Don't be so dramatic about it."

The words sounded from the far edges of Reed's consciousness. He wrapped his fingers around the grate and desperately attempted a push-up to dislodge his attacker. It was beyond futile—the weight on his back and the wire around his neck immobilized his core reflexes.

No way am I dying on this pier.

Reed pushed his head down with all the strength he could muster, digging the wire farther into his neck, but forcing The Wolf to lean forward. Then he shot his head back as hard and fast as he could, momentarily dislodging the choke wire from his throat and allowing him a sip of air.

It was enough.

Reed shoved down with his right arm and wrenched his shoulders to the left. The knee slid from the middle of his spine, and The Wolf toppled to the left, colliding with the grate as Reed slipped out of the choke wire. Torrents of vertigo sent Reed rocking back on his heels as he clawed at his jacket, searching for the revolver. The Wolf was already on his feet, spinning the long choke wire at the end of his fingers as he grinned and stepped toward Reed.

"You're just too good at staying alive."

Reed grabbed the gun by the end of the handle and tried to jerk it free of the holster, but it caught on the retention strap and refused to budge. He ducked a sweeping kick from The Wolf and dove toward the flags. His attacker followed, spinning the wire around his head like a lasso. Reed saw the choke wire coming toward him only an instant before it arced toward his head, and he stuck his arm up to shield himself from the noose.

The wire closed around his wrist, biting into his skin as The Wolf jerked backward. Reed grabbed the flag pole and yanked back, pulling on the wire and digging his toes into the metal grating.

The Wolf stumbled forward, the grin fading from his lips as Reed twisted, grabbed him by the collar, and lifted him over the rail. With one massive heave, Reed propelled the flailing assassin past the flags and over the railing. Metal screeched against metal as The Wolf plummeted toward the water, still clutching his end of the choke wire.

Oh shit.

The wire snapped tightly around Reed's wrist, and before he could regain his hold of the flagpole or dig his toes into the grate, The Wolf's full weight descended on his shoulder and snatched him forward, over the rail, and into midair beyond.

Both men crashed into the icy water. The wire jerked against Reed's wrist, pulling him deeper into the murk as his unseen enemy thrashed in the darkness somewhere nearby. His lungs throbbed, still starved for air, and he impulsively gulped down river water. Everything was black and cold, saturating his jacket and sinking straight into his bones.

The surface of the river broke over his face just in time to keep his lungs from collapsing on themselves. Reed sucked in a massive gulp of air and choked on water. The wire felt limp on his wrist now, and as he surveyed the surface of the river, he couldn't see The Wolf. Everything was eerily still next to the panicked chaos in Reed's mind. Nobody stood on the pier overhead, and no shouts of shock or offered assistance came from the riverbank. Only the wind filled his ringing ears, further numbing his chalky skin.

Where is he?

Fear overtook Reed's desire for blood, and he began to kick toward the shore. Mud closed over his boots only moments later, and he hauled himself onto the bank. Dry grass crumbled under his face as he fell forward, still panting for air. The water lapped at his ankles, and the wire still hung in a tangle around his wrist.

Picking himself up, Reed unwound the wire from his arm and flung it to the ground, then clawed at his jacket as he turned back to the lake. The comforting rubber grip of the revolver filled his hand, and he pried it free of the holster. All four inches of the massive barrel swung out, and Reed directed the muzzle toward the river. The water remained calm, with small ripples dancing against the shore as the river flowed slowly past.

Did he drown? No way.

Reed lowered the revolver and caught sight of something glimmering in the water twenty yards away. He leaned forward and squinted in the darkness, trying to making out the shape as it drifted closer to the shore. Trash? A body?

It's a stick.

The thought cleared his tired mind at the same moment a kneecap collided with his lower back. The revolver flew from his hand as the choke wire flashed over his eyes and clipped his chin before closing around his throat. Reed fell forward onto the bank, his chest crashing into the dirt as the full weight of his assailant descended on his back, and then his face was forced into the shallow water. The noose closed off his windpipe, cinching down so hard this time he imagined it slicing into his skin. Everything turned dark, and his eyes filled with dirty river water as his arms flailed against the shore.

There was no moving this time—no dislodging the killer perched on his back, jerking away at the wire. In a flash Reed saw distorted memories of prison. He saw Blazer—his first assassination on behalf of Oliver Enfield—from the far side of the prison fence. He heard his own voice as he lured his prey close to the fence, and then encircled the wire around Blazer's throat. He heard his victim cry out and struggle even as Reed snatched the wire back and twisted, slicing into his throat.

And this is how it ends.

The wire bit deeper into Reed's throat, and his windpipe closed off completely. The water covered his face, choking him, and the last tinges of panic faded from his body as his life continued to flash before him: his father, his mother, Baxter, Kelly . . . and Banks. Her face gleamed in his mind before the shadows engulfed him. A fading beep echoed in the distance, matching his slowing heart rate and slipping away into the far reaches of his consciousness. Then his entire body went limp.

11

Reed's ears hovered only half an inch over the water, allowing him to hear the distant electronic chirp.

Beep. Beep. Beep.

The wire loosened around his throat, and the weight fell off his back. His windpipe opened, but he was too weak to lift his face from the water. Only the darkness and the outline of Banks's fading features filled his mind.

Fingers closed around the collar of his jacket, and with a massive jerk, he was pulled out of the water and hurled onto the bank. His shoulders collided with the hard-packed earth, and water shot out of his throat as he gasped for air. The sky swirled overhead, twisting stars into streaks of lights that unleashed unprecedented surges of vertigo and nausea through his body. Reed coughed and spluttered on more river water, then felt concentrated pressure on the middle of his chest. He couldn't see the source of the weight but felt his ribs constrict and expand as the pressure increased, then alleviated.

Reed choked up more water, then sucked in a full breath of air. It whistled through his ragged and bruised throat, and his vision began to clear.

He coughed and fell over on his side. Black boots thumped against the ground only a few feet away, and the electronic beeping was suddenly silenced. Reed clawed his way into a sitting position and searched for the revolver as he rolled away from the boots.

"It's right here, dude."

The Wolf's voice sounded strained and breathless, but there was a hint of amusement in his tone. Reed rolled toward him and clenched his fingers into a fist, already raising his arms to defend himself.

Ten feet away, his assailant dripped with water and stared down at Reed. The choke wire dangled from his left hand, and Reed's massive .500 Magnum revolver hung from his right, but neither weapon was raised.

The Wolf curled the wire around his fingers, then twisted his neck until it popped. "You're one tough cookie, I'll give you that. Let the record state that I would have killed you."

Reed blinked back the water in his eyes. His throat hurt like hell, bruised and crushed by the weight of the wire, but his mind cleared as vital oxygen surged back into his brain.

"Why didn't you?" It was a stupid, pointless question, really. And yet the most obvious.

The Wolf ran a hand through his short hair, forcing the water out. His bright eyes glinted in the moonlight, a hint of mischief shining behind them.

"It's midnight. Didn't you hear my watch? I don't kill after business hours."

Reed sank his fingers into the sod, still fighting off the last traces of vertigo as he tried to compute what he just heard. Nothing made sense, and he tried to stand up.

"Well, I don't have business hours, so hand me that damn—"

"Don't curse." The Wolf lifted the revolver and wagged the muzzle toward Reed. "Or I might be inclined to reconsider my rules. And no, you're not getting this back. Just because I'm off the clock doesn't mean I'm going to let you kill me."

Reed stumbled to his feet. "Who the hell—"

"Uh-uh."

The muzzle of the revolver twitched again. Reed stumbled, almost collapsing as the world tilted beneath him. He vomited into the grass, a mixture of beer and bile splashing over his boots. His throat stung like hell.

"I see you've been eating well." There was more than a little derision in The Wolf's voice. Almost condescension.

Reed spat vomit from his mouth and straightened. "You listen here, you cheap shi—"

The hammer of the revolver clicked back, and the gaping barrel leveled over Reed's chest. The Wolf raised both eyebrows, and Reed sucked in a lungful of air. Stillness filled the space between them, and for a moment, Reed thought he would press the trigger. He could envision the blast of fire as the weapon belched thunder and hurled a thumb-sized chunk of lead straight through his heart.

The Wolf tilted his head and smirked, then lowered the hammer and shoved the revolver into his coat pocket.

"Kicking butt really awakens the munchies," he said. "I'm famished. By the look of it, you could use some sustenance yourself."

Reed relaxed his clenched fists. The Wolf kicked mud off his shoes, and then started up the hillside toward the city, two hundred yards away.

"Come along! I've got this outstanding spot a mile down the street. The onion rings are, simply put, absolutely scrumptious. And don't get me started on the *duck pâté en croûte.*"

Reed shot a glance around the riverside park. The commotion of two men thrashing around in the shallows, desperately trying to assassinate one another, hadn't garnered the attention of any locals. Only The Wolf stood on the bank, dripping water like a sopping dishrag as he started toward the city.

He's got my freaking gun.

The thought ignited strange, irrational anger inside of Reed. A basic instinct deep beneath the whistling breaths and aching chest told him he should be more concerned about his near-death experience, or perhaps it was the fact that the man who delivered that experience was himself still breathing. But somehow, the only thing that seemed pressingly important was the revolver jammed deep inside The Wolf's pocket. Reed felt like a kid whose favorite toy had been stolen on the playground. It was a deep, instinctive outrage.

Reed broke into a run up the hillside, wheezing and clutching his stomach the whole way. His head erupted with pain, making the shadows around him dance with every step, and his swollen throat throbbed as though a hot poker were being repeatedly rammed up and down it.

I'm going to rip his head off.

The Wolf walked in mechanical strides that kept him a dozen yards ahead. Reed followed him up the hill, where they walked past the anchored *Southern Belle* and then through the trees for a mile along the riverside. An occasional car drove by, headed toward downtown, but the streets were otherwise silent and shrouded in darkness.

"Now, understand." The Wolf spoke in a clear, chipper tone. "This place closes at midnight. I have an arrangement with the sous chef, a rather rotund fellow from the New England coast. Grills a cod on white rice like you wouldn't *believe.*"

The Wolf tilted his head back and groaned at the sky, then wagged his finger toward Reed. "Anyway, my point is, be polite. Rumor has it you have quite the temper. Dust off your manners or you can hit up White Castle."

Reed stumbled to a stop. He tried to speak past what was left of his throat, but the sound came out as a gurgle.

The Wolf lifted an eyebrow. "This is what I'm talking about. That's brutish."

The riverside restaurant was a small building constructed of cedar shingle siding with a metal roof and gas lighting on the exterior walls. The parking lot lay vacant except for a handful of cars in the employee parking section. The Wolf approached without any sign of hesitation and rapped twice on the front door.

Reed leaned on the wall and gasped for breath, his heart still pounding from the strangulation twenty minutes before. He eyed the bulge of the revolver in The Wolf's pocket and calculated the prospect of retrieving the weapon before The Wolf put him on the ground. It was beyond question now that Reed's hand-to-hand combat skills were far inferior, and whatever bizarre set of rules had prevented The Wolf from killing him before, Reed didn't think they would save him a second time. He would have to wait for the right moment.

The lock clicked, and the door swung open. A short Asian man with tiny glasses peered out, squinting at The Wolf a moment before a wide smile spread across his face. "Ah, Mr. Pierce! Such a pleasure. Please, come in."

The Wolf bowed, returned the greeting, then motioned Reed ahead. "After you, Mr. Montgomery."

Reed reluctantly slipped through the door and into the dimly lit restaurant. It was decorative—far more so than the humble exterior would have indicated. Gold trim lined the bar, and glistening chandeliers hung over the main dining room, casting dull pools of yellow over tables covered in soft white cloths. Staff bustled about the room, vacuuming the floors, replacing the tablecloths, and dusting the wall decor, but the Asian man motioned past the main dining room and led them to an alcove at the back of the restaurant with massive windows that overlooked the river. He bowed and gestured to a two-person table with large, leather-cushioned chairs.

"Please, have a seat. I'll let Alphonse know you're here. Would either of you care for a towel?"

Reed glanced down at the muddy river water pooling around his boots, then grunted and plopped down at the table. The host sighed and disappeared into the kitchen as Reed shot The Wolf a glare. "So, you've chased me through the mountains, tried to obliterate me with a minigun, strangled me within seconds of my life, and now apparently we're on a date. I think it's way past time you introduced yourself."

The Wolf sat down across from Reed and picked up a folded napkin from the table. He brushed the mud off his hands, then dabbed at his forehead before refolding it and replacing it on the table. "Fair enough. I'm Wolfgang Pierce, professionally known as *The Wolf*. I'm an assassin for hire."

Reed snorted. "Is that right? You know, I'm something of an assassin myself, only I actually kill people. I don't take them out for steak."

Wolfgang laughed. "Is that what you would've preferred? Because we can go back to the river, and I can drown you again."

Before Reed could answer, footsteps thumped against the carpet, and a short man with an immense potbelly appeared, dressed in a white apron with a floppy chef's hat perched atop his bald head. When the chef saw Wolfgang, his eyes lit up, and a smile spread across a mouth that contained less than half the usual ration of teeth.

"Mr. Pierce! What an unexpected delight. How go your studies?" Laden with a thick French accent, his babbled words almost blended together.

Wolfgang bowed and returned the smile. "Excellently, Alphonse. Thank you for asking. I actually graduated yesterday."

Alphonse snapped his fingers. "Ah, then it is *Doctor* Pierce!"

"Well, more or less. I still have a dissertation to write, but the diploma is secured, as it were. Alphonse, I'd like you to meet my colleague, Mr. Reed Montgomery, of Atlanta. He's joining me for dinner tonight."

Alphonse redirected his gaze at Reed, but instead of a bow and smile, his expression turned critical, and he folded his fingers over his gut.

Reed leaned back in his chair and scowled. "What the hell are you looking at?"

Wolfgang sighed. "Reed, if you curse again, I'll be forced to kill you."

Alphonse broke out into a raucous laugh and slapped himself on the leg. "That's funny," he said. "Because he actually kills people for a living!"

Wolfgang joined in on the merriment, smacking the table before wagging a finger at the chef. "Alphonse, you're *too much!* You'll have to forgive Reed. His manners are a great deal less refined than ours."

Reed switched his glare between Wolfgang and the chef. *What the hell is going on here?*

The Asian man appeared with a couple of rolled towels. Reed used one to wipe himself down as best he could, and Alphonse bowed again before bustling off to the kitchen. The Asian man introduced himself as David and offered to take their drink orders.

"I'll have black tea," Wolfgang said. "With a spoon of cream and a pinch of peppermint."

"Very good, sir. And you?"

"Whiskey," Reed said. "A lot of it."

David raised an eyebrow, but Wolfgang waved his hand dismissively, and the waiter retreated to the kitchen.

"I imagine you're thinking of a way to kill me," Wolfgang said, unfolding the cloth napkin and laying it over his lap.

"I just want my gun back."

"It's a little overkill, don't you think? .500 Magnum?"

"I could say the same about that Glock 10mm you tried to blow my brains out with back in North Carolina, you thug."

Wolfgang sighed. "Don't act so butthurt, Reed. It's only business. You should know that."

"You tried to run me over in a *Jeep,*" Reed snapped.

Wolfgang laughed and lifted his water glass. "I forgot about that. You run like a jackrabbit."

David returned to the table with a cup of tea on a saucer, and a small tumbler with two shots of whiskey on ice.

Reed drained the tumbler before it even hit the table and handed it back. "Bring the bottle."

Once again, David shot Wolfgang a sideways look, and Wolfgang nodded.

As soon as the waiter was out of earshot, Reed leaned across the table and glowered at Wolfgang. "All right, we're all impressed. You're fancy, refined, and the chef loves you. I want to know who hired you to kill me."

Wolfgang sipped his tea, then tapped a finger against the side of the cup. "Don't you know?"

"Would I have asked if I did?"

The teacup clicked back against the saucer, and Wolfgang stirred the jet-back tea with a silver spoon. "Usually, people know who they've crossed."

"Dude, I've crossed so many people, I've lost count. Any one of them could want me dead."

"Occupational hazard," Wolfgang said. "You certainly dealt with Oliver."

"I did. Along with his henchmen and the person who sold him those henchmen."

"Cedric Muri."

"Yes. Do you work for him?"

"Who? Muri? Absolutely not. I don't work for anyone. I'm a free agent."

Reed sneered. "Nobody's a free agent in this business. Everybody has a boss."

Wolfgang shook his head. "That's not true. I work for myself, take the jobs I want, decline the jobs I don't. It leaves me plenty of free time to pursue my interests."

"Isn't that nice." Reed crossed his arms. "I'm sorry if I seem cold, but you *did* try to strangle me just a moment ago, and you also tried to kill somebody very important to me. I'm not in the mood for banter."

"If you're talking about Banks Morccelli, you should know that I would've never hurt her. The grenades were necessary to dislodge you off the cliff, but you were the one who put her in harm's way. I cannot be responsible for collateral damage when you use women as human shields."

Reed's blood boiled, and he slammed a closed fist against the table, sending silverware raining down over the floor. Wolfgang didn't react, but sat with the teacup in one hand and stared at Reed.

"Did you do it?" Reed hissed. "Did you burn Kelly?"

Wolfgang set the cup down, wiped his mouth, then shook his head. "No, I didn't. I would never kill somebody that way."

"But you'd blow them up with a minigun. You'd gun them down in a coffee shop."

Wolfgang stared off with vacant eyes, as though he had left the restaurant, and his mind was now far away. "Reed, I don't want to compare rap sheets. We've both done some unspeakable things, and we've both had our reasons. As an independent contractor, I operate under my own rules. One of those rules is that I don't kill people between midnight and six a.m. That's my choice. I would enjoy a civil dinner with you, one professional to another, but I'm not going to continue tolerating these outbursts."

Reed's breaths hissed through his swollen throat. He accepted a full glass of whiskey from David and drained it, deadening the ache of developing bruises on his body. The preposterousness of Wolfgang's erratic behavior didn't register with him. The Wolf was eclectic in the extreme, and perhaps he had reason to be. Or maybe he was simply weird. Either way, Reed couldn't kill him right now, and he wasn't going to wait around for Wolfgang to kill him.

Reed stood up, dropping the towel on the table. "Tell your boss, whoever the *hell* he is, that I'm coming for him. I'm coming for them all."

Wolfgang twisted the teacup in his hand. His fingers turned white against the porcelain, and for a moment, Reed almost thought he saw sympathy, but that light faded, replaced by iron and darkness.

"I'm sorry to hear that, Reed. I'm sorry we fell on opposite sides of the ditch. You're a good killer, and if you allowed yourself, you might even be a good man. But next time I see you, I'm going to kill you."

Their gazes locked, steel clashing against steel, and Reed walked out of the restaurant without another word.

12

Lake Maurepas, Louisiana

Maggie never liked the governor's mansion. Large, over-decorated, and inspired by all things plantation, the official residence of Louisiana's executive leader was downtown, only a couple miles from the Capitol. It wasn't that she didn't appreciate the grandeur and status of the luxury residence, and she certainly enjoyed the private chef and quiet study, but it just didn't feel like home. It was too fancy, filled with too many breakable things, and altogether too clean.

Most nights, Maggie was forced to sleep at the residence by virtue of its proximity to the Capitol. Late-night paperwork and administrative tasks kept her at her official office until midnight or later, and early-morning meetings began as soon as the sun crested over the mighty Mississippi. But some nights, when the workload bore too heavy on her tired shoulders, she slipped away from the crowds of aides and media reporters and took a long drive south of the city, into the swamplands of Louisiana.

The old family lake house sat on the shores of Lake Maurepas, a brackish catfish lake with an average depth of fewer than ten feet. People from out of town found the lake to be both smelly and ugly, but Maggie loved the calm and simplicity of the swampy landscape. Frogs croaked in the darkness, the wind rustled through the grass, and the occasional alligator crawled past the back porch, migrating from one muddy inlet to the next. It was home, even if it felt less private with the burly state policeman standing guard outside.

As the sun melted into the pines, the moon took over, filling the night sky with a blue glow that reminded Maggie of late-night 'coon hunting with her father. When she closed her eyes, she could still hear the howl of the hounds and the crash of the brush as the two barged ahead, shotguns at the ready, alive in the hunt.

She missed everything about those simple days. When she went to law school and first considered running for political office, it was out of frustration more than passion. After years of watching corruption in Baton Rouge overrun the simple, low-income families of her community, she wanted to make a statement—defy the system.

Funny how such a small spark could ignite a wildfire. And it wasn't just the people around her who burst into flames—Maggie herself became consumed with the campaign. The more she learned about the status quo in Louisiana's capital, the more frustrated she became, and the harder she campaigned. Her only goal had been to pressure the older, more mature candidates into appreciating the needs of her neighbors.

By the time she won the nomination, it was too late to turn back. Even when she accepted the concession call from her opponent on election night, she still clung to the hope that after a single term, she could have accomplished enough to hand the reins over to someone else and open the small community law practice that she always dreamed of. She wanted to live a simple life—be the friend of the people.

Those fantasies were long dead now. Baton Rouge was a machine—a vortex that pulled you in and pulled you down, regardless of the odds. She still didn't want to be there, but she believed more than ever that it was her responsibility to serve the people, and that obligation chained her down.

Maggie sat on the edge of her bed, and through her narrow window, watched the moon glinting off the water. Every few minutes, her guard would pass by, a shotgun swinging from one hand. Fish splashed from the lake's surface, conducting elaborate flips before vanishing into the murky water again. Everything was so calm.

She sighed and closed her eyes. Her dreams were selfish. She knew that. Her old man would be ashamed of her if he knew how badly she wanted to throw in the towel after only five months of serving as governor. There was still work to be done—still justice to be served.

"A Trousdale never quits." Her father said it a thousand times. It was her mantra and what pushed her through college and brought her out of law school. Surrendering was never an option.

Maggie lay back on the bed, kicking off her flats and resting her head against a worn pillow. It was cheap, like everything in the cabin. This was the mansion of the minimum wage—the palace of a working-class family. Nothing was nice, but everything was wonderful.

A creaking sound erupted from down the hall. Maggie's eyes snapped open, and she held her breath, listening carefully. She recognized that distinct grunt. It was the sound the third floorboard in the hallway made when somebody stepped on it. She used to avoid that board when she was a teenager and snuck out at night to meet her boyfriend by the lake. It was a unique sound—one she shouldn't have heard in an empty house.

She turned and looked out the window, still holding her breath while she waited for her guard to walk by, but he didn't pass. Only the wind rustled through the grass.

Then she heard it again.

Maggie set her feet on the floor and opened the nightstand drawer. An old Colt .38 Special revolver lay in the bottom, a thin layer of dust clinging to the metal cylinder. She depressed the release switch and checked the five bullets housed within before snapping the cylinder shut and creeping toward the door. Her fingers trembled, and sweat pooled on her lip. She wasn't sure if it was her imagination, but she thought she heard heavy breaths on the other side of the door and a faint scuffling sound, like a boot scraping a baseboard.

Maggie ducked into the shadows behind the door and held the revolver next to her ear. A few seconds dripped by, and the guard still didn't pass outside. She heard the soft squeak of metal on metal, and the doorknob twisted.

Her heart flew into her mouth, and she inserted a shaking index finger through the trigger guard. The knob twisted again, and the latch clicked, then the door swung open on silent, greased hinges, and a single black boot landed on the floor without a sound.

Maggie's stomach twisted, and her head felt light. She recognized the dull grey color of the pants with soft gold trim. The boots were the standard issue of the Louisiana State Police. As the intruder took another step into the room, she recognized the broad shoulders and short blond hair.

It was Officer Maxwell. The lead guard of her nighttime detail.

Maggie lowered the revolver, her arms growing steady as she watched Maxwell walk away from her, toward the bed. An unholstered pistol hung from his right hand, reflecting moonlight from its polished black barrel. The bed was saturated in shadows, disguising the presence, or absence, of anyone sleeping within, and forcing Maxwell to take another step.

Maggie cocked the revolver. The splitting click of the weapon shattered the stillness like a thunderclap. Maxwell froze as Maggie took a step out of the darkness and leveled the weapon's barrel with the back of his head.

"Turn around."

Maxwell turned slowly, the gun shaking in his right hand. As he faced her, the clouds parted, spilling light over his face and exposing his features. Maggie gasped and lowered the weapon. Blood covered his cheeks and streamed from a deep cut in his chest. His face was washed white, and his eyes were as wide and dark as the lake outside.

He took half a step forward and dropped the gun, stumbling to his knees. "Madam Governor . . . we have to go." His words broke and hissed between his teeth. A trail of blood oozed from between his lips and dripped on the floor.

Maggie slid to her knees beside him and caught the big policeman as he toppled forward. His weight was almost overwhelming, but she managed to prop him up against the end of the bed. He gasped for air, his body still shaking as she held him.

"Maxwell, where's Green?"

Maggie saw worlds of pain and fear unleashed behind Maxwell's watering eyes.

"Madam Governor, I'm so sorry . . . I couldn't . . . stop him."

"It's okay." Maggie placed her hand over the wide gash in his chest and pressed down, wadding his torn shirt into the wound. She jerked the radio from his side and hit the call button.

"Is anyone there?"

There was no response, and Maggie cursed before depressing it again. "I said, is anyone listening?"

The radio crackled. "This is a secure government line. Identify yourself."

"This is Maggie Trousdale. I'm at my lake house. One of my guards is missing, and the other is bleeding. I need immediate medical assistance."

"Who now?"

"I'm the governor, you dumb shit! Get some help out here!"

A snapping sound rang from outside the house, and Maggie's back stiffened as she looked up toward the window. Clouds blew across the moon, drenching the house in shadow. Among the outlines of tree limbs and bushes, she saw something hard and straight—too mechanical to be natural.

Maxwell was unconscious now, his eyes rolled back in his head. She laid him down and scooped up the revolver before ducking through the doorway and hurrying down the hallway. Her bare feet smacked against the hardwood, and the third floorboard squeaked as she stepped out of the hallway and into the kitchen.

The front door hung half-open, and bloody handprints coated the doorjamb. As Maggie crept closer and pulled the door back, her heart jumped again. Green, her second LSP guard, lay dead on the front porch, his throat sliced open.

Just past the porch, Maggie saw a shadow out of the corner of her eyes. She spun the revolver toward it and pressed the trigger without aiming. The little .38 cracked and spat a bullet into the darkness. After a scream of pain, something clattered onto the pinewood boards of the porch. Maggie lunged out from the doorway and fired twice more. Sticks and rocks dug into her feet as she stumbled into the mud. Heavy breathing carried through the fog, somewhere amid the sound of rustling grass and crunching twigs. The thick stench of blood invaded her nostrils as warm mud squished between her toes. Ahead, she could see the silhouette of a man running through the trees, holding his side.

Maggie raised the gun. "Stop!"

The shadow kept running, diving for the cover of the pines. Maggie aligned the sights of the snub-nosed revolver, cocked the hammer, and squeezed the trigger. The bullet split the air and sent a shockwave of burned gunpowder blasting back over her hand, but the running man didn't stop. In an instant, the darkness consumed him, leaving her standing alone over the bloody ground.

As the gunshot faded, the whisper of the wind filled the stillness, rendering everything empty and dark. Maggie dug her fingernails into the grip of the gun and searched the forest. Only shadows filled the spaces between the trees, consuming her with the gripping reality that she was alone, and they would be back.

13

———

"It's a lot smaller than home, isn't it, boy?"

Baxter's legs were splayed out over the passenger seat as he pressed his flat face close to the window and peered out at the city. Trucks and cars whizzed past the Camaro, cutting in and out from each other as they surged toward downtown.

Nashville looked nothing like Atlanta. The skyline was half as wide, with shorter buildings all made of glass and shiny metal. It was a new skyline—the kind a millennial designed. The bulk of downtown was dominated by the thick, impending mass of the AT&T Building, a circular tower that culminated in a narrow, flat top, and twin spires that reached for the sky like bat ears.

It was a nice skyline, but Reed thought it lacked the grandeur and majesty of Atlanta. It was too young—too polished.

And still too large a place to locate a single woman.

Reed followed the bypass around downtown, admiring the open hulk of Nissan Stadium before exiting the freeway onto 2nd Avenue. Reed knew very little about this city, other than that it had recently gained a reputation as a tourist destination for bars and live music. Nashville supposedly now boasted the title of "Number One Bachelorette Destination of the Nation."

And isn't that every city's dream?

Reed drove only two blocks into downtown before the first Pedal Tavern crossed the street ahead of him—a peculiar table-on-wheels contraption with riders on both sides working pedals that propelled the bar through the streets. The passengers were drunk, at barely noon. He didn't make it another two blocks before he passed a tractor towing a wagon full of drunk women in their twenties, a modified fire truck with an open top, filled with the same, and more than a dozen peculiar electric scooters laden with overweight tourists. Reed had never seen so much crap on the streets—golf carts, Pedal Taverns, modified pickup trucks with extended beds full of partiers, open-top school buses with disco lights. Even some type of modified RV with a hot tub in the back, filled with bachelorettes. The bizarre assortment of vehicles and drunk tourists bridged beyond unusual into the obscene.

What the hell is this place?

The Camaro barked and rumbled as he swerved around a pack of scooters and moved deeper into the city. People—old, young, of every race and origin—were everywhere, packed onto the sidewalks and jostling each other between the bars. Reed wondered if this was typical of a Friday, and what this place must look like after dark.

With any luck, I'll never find out.

Reed used to enjoy crowded places. He remembered car shows and trips to Disneyland as a kid. They took the old Camaro everywhere as a family, and he relished the excitement of people packed into one place. All that changed when he stopped seeing other people as fellow tourists and started suspecting them of being fellow killers. In a place like this, thick with every type of traveling amusement seeker, any number of foreign threats could slip right in, and nobody would be any the wiser.

But this is where she is. This is the first place Banks would go. Lots of people to lose herself in. Lots of music to block out the world.

He pulled the car into a parking lot and cut the engine, watching the tides of people washing back and forth across the sidewalks. Two blocks down, the bright neon signs of the bar district connected 2nd Avenue with

Broadway. More people packed in next to a string of bars and restaurants, clamoring against each other to gain access. Even through the Camaro's thick windows, the roar of voices was overwhelming, melding with the pound of a few rock bands performing on the other side of open windows.

Baxter snorted as he peered through the windshield with stress-filled eyes.

"I know, boy. Crowds aren't for us, are they?"

Reed rubbed the key between his fingers and forced out the cloud of emotions that tugged at the edge of his thought process.

Should I be here? Would she be safer if I left her alone?

He thought again of the last time he saw her, soaking wet and crying on the lake bank. She didn't deserve what happened to her in those mountains, but if it weren't for him, she probably would've died there. Sure, it could be argued that he kicked things off when he accepted the Holiday contract in the first place, but it could also be argued that Holiday was going to die anyway. Somebody, somewhere, wanted the senator dead. Reed just gave them more trouble than most.

If I don't find her now, I'll never have a chance to make this right.

"Get in the back, boy. Don't want somebody thinking you're abandoned and busting out my windows."

Reed cracked both windows as Baxter grunted and climbed into the back seat. It was sixty degrees outside, and with the fresh air streaming through the windows, Baxter would be comfortable and safe until he returned.

The crowd melded around Reed as soon as he stepped onto the sidewalk, accepting him as one of their own and crushing in so close several of them bumped into his arms. Reed held his jacket close over the compact SIG Sauer P365 holstered in his belt. The little 9mm held only ten rounds—far too little firepower for his comfort. After losing most of his primary weaponry in North Carolina, and then the revolver in Chattanooga, Reed was left with nothing but his backup weapon, and he felt altogether undergunned. After he left Nashville, he would need to refit—find a broker and secure new hardware.

His boots splashed through mud puddles as he worked his way toward Broadway. Every bar he passed stood with wide-open doors and a heavy bouncer checking IDs at the sidewalk. Half a dozen types of music drifted through the air—pop, rock, country, classics, and even a little blues. All of the bands were good, and what vocals joined the mix were considerably better than average.

They don't call it Music City for nothing, I guess.

Reed followed the crowd through the crosswalk and onto Broadway. On his right, the street dropped down toward the Cumberland River, lined by restaurants on both sides. What stretched out on his left really took his breath away. Three solid blocks of three-story bars packed door-to-door. Lights, signs, and decor clung to the exterior brick walls while hundreds of people surged up and down either side of the street. Taxis, Ubers, and police cars jockeyed for position along the four-lane road, with more Pedal Taverns sprinkled amongst them. A horn blared, and Reed looked to his right just in time to jump out of the way of a green tractor towing a hay wagon full of drunk women, all swaying and singing *"Oh Canada"* at the top of their lungs.

What the hell is this?

There were too many bars, dozens of them, all stacked and packed together, and that was only on this street. Each connecting road boasted more signs pointing to additional bars and restaurants that clustered outside of Broadway.

This could take days. She could be anywhere.

Reed pulled himself away from the crush of people and leaned against a brick wall, taking a moment to survey the city. It made sense for Banks to be in a place that celebrated music this much. He wondered how many of these bands were regular attractions, and how many rotated new acts.

She'll be somewhere that hires new talent, where she can sing for tips like she did in Atlanta.

"Excuse me." Reed stepped toward a cop who stood on the corner. "Do you live here?"

The officer shot Reed a sour look. "Unfortunately," he said. "What can I help you with?"

"I'm looking for a place to sing. Someplace that takes new talent."

The cop burst out laughing. He paused a moment to blow his whistle and shout at a speeding taxi, then turned back to Reed and laughed again. "You and forty thousand others. I'm not a record agent, bro."

"Let me clarify. A friend of mine is the new talent. She came up here to sing, and I forgot the name of the bar."

The officer blew his whistle again and waved his hand at a couple of kids zooming past on a pair of electric scooters. They ignored him, and he threw his hands into the air. "Damn kids!"

Reed cleared his throat. "So, about the bar . . ."

"Try Sweeney's. It's on Third Avenue past FGL."

Reed nodded his thanks and stepped off as the cop resumed the whistle blowing. One block down and two to the left, clinging to the side of a building, was a large black sign with white letters: FGL HOUSE.

Just beyond it, "Sweeney's Saloon" was painted in gold letters on red brick. It was a narrow bar with the sort of old swinging doors that you see in cowboy movies. The bouncer blocking the doorway was big, fat, and appeared totally stoned, but he demanded Reed's ID.

Reed displayed a fake South Carolina driver's license labeled "Christopher Thomas," then ducked into the bar. It was smoky and dark inside, with tables crammed together along both walls. Servers jumped from one table to the next, handing out beers and glasses of liquor, while a scrawny kid with long, greasy hair groaned into the microphone at the stage in the back.

Reed helped himself to a chair in the corner, leaning against the wall and inhaling a deep lungful of second-hand smoke. It took the edge off his nerves but ignited an almost overwhelming urge to smoke. He hadn't enjoyed a cigarette in days.

Nobody paid the kid at the mic any attention. His style was weak, with words strung together and overwhelmed by moans that sounded more like the overtures of a masturbating teenager than a vocalist. Reed eyed him and thought how strange it was to be in a place where so many people were hungry for the limelight. He never understood that. Power made sense to him, and so did money. These were tangible, actionable resources. But fame? Who wanted to be famous? Reed had spent the better part of his life trying to keep most of the world from knowing anything about him. Clamoring for attention didn't make sense.

The kid at the mic finally finished and dismounted the stage to a few scattered claps.

A dusty bartender in torn-out jeans and a black T-shirt got up behind him and spoke into the mic. "Let's put it together for Rebel Joe!"

This time, the scattered claps were a little louder but no more enthusiastic.

"All right, you guys. I know you're ready to get your country on. We've got one more independent act—"

From the back of the room, somebody bellowed, "Put on some real music!"

The bartender pointed at him and smiled. "Take it easy, friend. We'll have somebody up in just a moment. Y'all go ahead and order another round!"

The radio clicked on overhead, pounding a popular country song through oversized speakers as a server slipped up beside Reed. "Can I get you something to drink, honey?"

Reed's eyes darted from one corner of the room to the next, searching for any unseen threats amongst the tourists. He replied without looking up. "Got any whiskey?"

She laughed. "Honey, this is Tennessee. We brush our teeth with whiskey."

"I'll take a Jack. Neat."

"Coming right up."

She disappeared into the crowd, and Reed folded his arms. The bustle and noise brought comfort to his ragged mind. It made him feel a little less conspicuous amid all these people. It made him feel like there was a chance he could shrink away and not be seen at all.

The server brought the whiskey, and Reed sipped on it, still watching the crowd. Wolfgang would be back. More than likely, the killer had already left Chattanooga and was headed his way, blazing down the road in his big Mercedes.

I've got to tie that one up. He's been on my heels far too long.

The whiskey tasted weak on his tongue, as though it were cut with water. Or maybe he was still drunk from the previous night. He tipped the glass up and drained it, then dusted off his pants. He couldn't afford to wait around for what probably wouldn't happen. There had to be a better way to find Banks.

"All right, ladies and gentlemen. I've got a special treat for you all the way from Atlanta, Georgia. Put your hands together for Miss Sirena Wilder!"

Reed's gaze flew to the stage. Ripples of polite applause rose from the audience as the radio faded, and the lights dimmed. His own eyes blurred, maybe from the saturation of alcohol in his blood, or the residual effects of insomnia, but he blinked the fog away and held his breath.

Please . . .

She stepped out of the darkness behind the stage, floating across the hardwood floor. A ghost of grace and beauty, her blonde waves were held back in a ponytail, and an acoustic guitar swung from a strap around her neck.

Her eyes, so deep and bright. But Reed could see the pain in them, carefully hidden, masked behind strength and willpower. Even her insatiable ability to manage stress and ignore trauma couldn't defeat the red streaks and black circles. Heavy makeup—dark eyeliner with bright red lipstick—coated her face, and she wore a loose T-shirt with sleeves that hung almost to her elbows.

Banks leaned close to the mic and smiled. Reed remembered the last time he saw her on a stage, leaning into a mic. She smiled then, too, but it wasn't like this smile. It was free and weightless—the smile that stole his heart in a millisecond.

"How's it going, Nashville?"

The room cheered. A couple tables away, Reed heard a drunk guy lean in and grunt to his friend, "Damn dawg. I'd hit that."

Banks strummed her fingers across the guitar strings, unleashing a gentle melody into the room. Reed recognized it immediately, and it flooded him with aching memories of that bar in Atlanta—the first place he heard those chords. As Banks leaned forward and pressed her lips next to the mic, a new wave of guilt and passion swept over him.

"He was a vagrant, and I a gypsy. I lost my way when he first kissed me."

Reed looked away from the stage. The wrenching agony that cascaded through his whole body felt more real and painful than any fistfight or bullet wound. It was total, complete heartache.

I did this to her.

The bar sat in transfixed silence as Banks sang. The boisterous drunks in the back watched with their glassy, intoxicated gazes fixed on the singer as she whispered each delicate lyric into the mic. Nobody moved. Nobody talked. Banks enraptured them as much as she had enraptured him only four weeks prior.

But this time, he could tell the difference. He detected the missing passion, the cavern behind the words. Banks was too much a performer to relax on her delivery, but she couldn't fake the emptiness in her voice.

"Can I get you another?" Reed was suddenly aware of the waitress at his side, leaning close. He blinked away the fog in his eyes and shook his head. She turned and wandered off through the crowd, leaving him alone as Banks broke into the bridge.

"I give, I gave, I'd have given him everything. I just wanted to believe some things would last forever."

Each word shredded what remained of his stamina, emotionally bringing him to his knees. He didn't recall her singing this bridge in Atlanta, though perhaps it was a lapse in memory or the alcohol fogging his brain. Or maybe he had crushed her even deeper than he had crushed himself.

Banks's soft voice drifted away, and for a moment, Reed forgot about all the people pressed in around him. Then a wave of roaring applause filled the room, shaking the walls and pounding in his ears. Banks smiled, her bright lips lifting into what *looked* like true happiness, but he could see past the mask, through the charade of a performer. Her real smile could light up a tomb, and this wasn't it.

She played three more songs, all covers of popular country tracks, then she waved and bowed without a word and moved toward the back of the building. Reed dropped a twenty on the table, then pushed his way through the crowd and out the swinging doors. The chaos of the city streets crushed in around him as he forced his way along the sidewalk, fighting around the building to the nearest alley. Piles of pallets and empty alcohol boxes lined the walls as he pushed through them, splashing across mud puddles and around dumpsters to the back of the three-story bar and the connecting alley.

As he rounded the corner, he saw her. Banks sat on the back step next to a closed door, her guitar leaned up against the brick wall and her head in her hands as her shoulders rose and fell in gentle sobs. His world stood still, locked in a purgatory of her tears. Every protective and loving instinct within him ignited, thundering to life and commanding him to rush forward, take her in his arms, and sweep her off her feet.

But he couldn't move. His feet were frozen to the ground, locked down by guilt and uncertainty. He swallowed back the dryness in his throat and whispered, "Banks . . ."

Her blue eyes flashed as they met his. The cloud of confusion and hurt that filled her gaze clamped down on him, unleashing new levels of pain. She stood up and stepped back. Her hair, now a tangled mess hanging over her ears and eyes, was stuck to her forehead by a layer of sweat.

It's sixty degrees outside. Why is she sweating?

Reed took a step forward. "I need to talk to you."

She licked her lips, her face flushing a sudden crimson, and she shook her head once, then took another step back.

"Please." Reed waited, still holding out his hand.

She hesitated, and her lips parted. For a moment, he thought she was about to speak, but then he noticed her chest heaving in short puffs. Her flushed face faded to a pale white, and without a sound, she collapsed in the alley.

14

Salvador hated America with every part of his soul. Deep within him, in his very bones, this place felt hostile and cold. Maybe it was because of his line of work, or because he was hostile and cold himself. Maybe it was because America made him into a person he never wanted to be.

The darkness of the small hotel room hung around him like a cloak, and the lights from his laptop danced in front of his eyes. The video feed was weak and broken, shifting and freezing from time to time, but the audio was clear. The familiar voices of his family, four thousand miles away in the midst of war-torn Venezuela, carried over the fickle internet connection, bringing the first warmth to his soul that he had felt in weeks. A smile spread across his tired face as the voice of his grandmother babbled on in hurried Spanish, discussing the local politics that ravaged his homeland. He listened to the words, but the only thing he heard was the voice. His sisters, two nephews, and his mother also appeared on the screen in turns, excitedly greeting him with smiles and blown kisses. Salvador waved back and asked them about school, work, and what books his mother was reading. Salvador sent books home every week for her, along with his weekly wire transfers. He could see the warmth in their cheeks and a little fat beneath their olive skin for the first time in months. Food was hard to come by in Venezuela, as inflation and political turmoil shattered the weak economy. The money Salvador sent home was the only thing keeping his large family alive. It was why he left South America in the first place—to find a lifeline that would keep his hungry siblings in school and his parents and grandparents out of the grave.

"How are things at the plant, Salvador?" His mother put down the book she had been reading to him and smiled with the sort of warmth and love that only a mother could express.

Salvador hesitated. "The plant . . . yes. Things are well. We're building parts for Nissan."

"Are you still enjoying the work? Are they treating you well?"

Salvador smiled. "Of course, Mamá. Things are different in America. The factories are safe."

"They pay you so much. It's hard to understand."

He shrugged. "I work hard for them. They give me extra hours."

The smile faded from her wrinkled lips, and worry crowded into her eyes. "Salvador, you don't have to. You should be pursuing your own life. Finding a nice girl. All this work is going to kill you."

Salvador shrugged. "I enjoy the work, Mamá. You know that. Is Papá home?"

The worry in her eyes faded to sadness, but she nodded. The laptop twisted, and the screen froze, then it was filled with the familiar features of his tired father—worn and serious. Salvador had never seen his father smile—not once in thirty-two years. He was more than a serious man; he was a severe one. But he loved his family, and he would do anything to protect them.

"Papá, how are you?"

The old man grunted. "I'm fine, Salvador. How are things at the '*plant*'?" Salvador's father never spoke of the plant without suspicion in his tone. Every time he asked about the work in America, his eyebrows furrowed, and he stared at Salvador with the intensity of a man who didn't believe anything he was being told. Maybe he saw through Salvador's farce, or maybe it was simply sixty years of programed distrust for America talking. Venezuela was, after all, a communist-leaning nation and a loose ally with the Soviet Union during the Cold War.

Salvador shifted but smiled. "Well, Papá, I'm getting promoted soon. I'll be able to send more home to the family."

His father grunted. "We don't need the money, Salvador. I can provide for the family on my own."

"The children need schoolbooks, and Mamá needs medicine for her back. I'm happy to help."

The suspicion in the old man's eyes remained, but he shrugged. The video feed faded and froze again, but the distorted audio continued to carry through the tiny laptop speakers.

"Salvador, there's something I want you to know."

The audio cut and warbled with electronic distortion. Salvador leaned closer to the computer, holding his ear next to the speaker. He still couldn't hear anything.

"Papá? Are you there?"

" . . . I know . . . I should have . . ."

The screen went black, and then a window popped up: VIDEO CALL FAILED.

Salvador closed the laptop. He ran his hands through his dark hair as exhaustion tore at his mind. It wasn't the kind that comes from the physical exertion he claimed to expend at the plant. This was the exhaustion of mental torment, months of self-doubt, and guilt. So much damn guilt.

He didn't want to become a killer. He didn't leave Venezuela to administer violence elsewhere. He came here to find better work and to find a way to feed his starving family. But the immigration system rejected him. He was deported twice, returning to Venezuela without visiting his parents or letting them know of his failures. Embarrassment and self-hatred wouldn't allow him to fail, and it soon became clear that if he wanted to get ahead in the world—if he wanted to win—he had to fight dirty.

The criminal underworld was a cold and ruthless place, but working for men who lived in the shadows paid a great deal better than any Nissan plant ever would. Salvador was good at making things happen. He was good at being the hand of men who couldn't afford to leave fingerprints. Being the fingerprint himself, and risking his own demise, promised the payout his family depended on.

Salvador twisted until his back crackled. He picked up a photograph from the desk and walked through the connecting door to the adjoining suite. Six men stood around a table loaded with MP5 submachine guns and H&K pistols. Dressed in black combat gear, they were pale-skinned, broad-shouldered, Swedish by birth, and a solid eight inches taller than him: trained killers, all of them. The six men were members of the East European mercenary group, Legion X. After Cedric Muri was gunned down in Atlantic City, Salvador knew he might need backup, so he hired Legion X out of his own pocket, flew them into Atlanta, and now held them in reserve.

A seventh man lounged in a chair in the corner of the room. Unlike the others, he wore street clothes and tennis shoes, and his blonde hair stuck out from under an Atlanta Braves hat.

Salvador raised an eyebrow. "Well?"

The man in the corner nodded. He spoke in a heavy Swedish accent with weak English, but Salvador could make out the gist of what he was saying. "It is as you said. He did not kill Montgomery. They fought near the river, then The Wolf just . . . quit. I do not know why."

Salvador nodded. "We have work to do. Two of you are flying to New York immediately. There's a young woman at a special needs facility outside of Buffalo. Pick her up and take her to Detroit. Don't harm her, and wait for further instructions."

Salvador dropped the photograph on the table. It was of a young woman with dark hair. Her eyes were bright, but her cheeks pale. Her body thin. A lifetime spent fighting a chronic illness had taken its toll.

One of the men in black picked up the photo and regarded it through narrowed eyes. "Who is this woman?"

Salvador walked to the window and crossed his arms, staring out at the city. His stomach knotted, but he swallowed back the taste of bile in his mouth. "Her name is Collins. She's The Wolf's sister. If we cannot pay the man to do his job, we'll force him."

15

Reed sat next to the narrow bed and stroked Banks's forehead with a damp washcloth. Her face had faded from white to red, and now back to white. Her skin was warm to the touch, and her palms were clammy. When he held his ear against her chest, he heard her heart thump at an accelerated pace. Banks inhaled in short gusts and breathed out just as fast.

He dipped the washcloth back into the bowl and wrung it out before touching it to her forehead again. Her nose twitched, and her head turned a little, but she didn't open her eyes.

Baxter lay on the floor next to him, drool pooling on the carpet beside his slack jaw. The bulldog's legs were splayed out behind him, but his eyes peered up at Reed with concern rippling through their inky depths.

Reed wiped the cloth across his own forehead. He wasn't sure why he confronted Banks in the alley behind the bar. He had to find her—that thought rang clearly through his head from the moment he accepted Kelly's death and drove away from the scene of the fire. For two weeks he searched diligently to locate Banks, hiring Dillan and implementing every Google search known to man. It was a fruitless, desperate search—something that consumed his every thought outside of destroying the people who murdered Kelly.

Now that he found her, he wasn't entirely sure why he started looking in the first place. Deep within his soul, he felt things for this woman that he had never felt for anyone. He cared for her in an instinctive, meaningful way that regulated his actions and filtered his intentions right to their core. But none of those feelings answered the dominating question of why he felt he had the authority to track her down. Did she deserve her privacy? Should he have let her go?

Baxter grunted, almost as though he understood Reed's internal conflict better than Reed understood it himself.

I can't let her go. I have to make this right.

Banks stirred, and Reed sat up. She had lain passed out on the bed for four hours now, with occasional twitches. But this time, her eyes fluttered, and her tongue touched her dry lips.

"Here, drink this." He held out a bottle of water with a straw.

Her eyes were still clouded with confusion as she accepted the straw and sucked down two greedy gulps of water, then fell back against the pillow. She blinked and turned her head toward him. "Chris."

Reed looked away, fiddling with the rag in the bowl.

She lay still, but he heard her breathing regulate as her full consciousness returned. Her voice turned cold as she spoke again. "No. Not Chris. *Reed.*"

Reed folded the towel around his fingers, refusing to face her. Banks pushed her hands beneath her and began to sit up.

"You should lay down," Reed said. "You need to rest."

"I know what I need," she snapped. She leaned against the wall and grabbed the water bottle. Reed thought she might have intended to snatch it from him, but she was too weak to give it more than a tug. He released it, and she gulped down two more swallows.

"I'm home."

"Yes." Reed cast a glance around the tiny apartment. It was a studio with dingy yellow walls and carpet that somehow rivaled that of the hotel in Chattanooga.

"How did you find my place?"

Reed gestured to her phone. "Significant location on your maps app."

"My phone was locked." There was no grace in her voice. No feeling.

Reed shrugged. "Thumbprint."

"Nice. Glad to see you're still busy intruding."

Reed forced himself to face her, then rested his palms against his kneecaps and cleared his throat. "Are you . . . okay?"

Banks pushed sweaty hair out of her eyes and tilted her head. "Well, let me see. The man I thought loved me turned out to be a liar, a psychopath, a professional killer, and the kidnapper of my godfather—who, by the way, was brutally gunned down right in front of me. I have no family left, no friends, I'm living in this shithole trying to be left alone, and now *you're* here. How do you *think* I'm doing?"

Reed rubbed his fingers against his worn jeans, then took a slow breath. "I meant . . . physically. You seem sick."

Banks blew a fallen strand of hair out of her eyes. "Wow, you're a regular Sherlock Holmes, aren't you?"

"I know you have Lyme disease."

"Oh, do you now? Well, that shouldn't surprise me. You are, after all, a black-hearted criminal. Bet you know all kinds of things."

Reed looked away. Her every word bit like a knife, tearing into him. Igniting more pain than any of his dozens of injuries over the last two weeks. He wanted to spill his guts. Tell her everything about Iraq and prison and the bad choices he made that led him down this long, bloody path. Explain himself.

But no. She wouldn't buy any of it. The proof was in the pudding, after all, and the only pudding she had ever seen was the blood and carnage he'd left behind.

"I can't apologize for what I've done," he said. "I don't think there's anything I can say that will make it better. I'm willing to tell you anything you want to know. I'm asking you to believe me when I say I never meant for you to get hurt. I did everything in my power to protect you."

Banks snorted. "Well, aren't I a lucky girl?"

Reed looked up again. "You don't even know what happened . . . why your godfather was killed."

"Does it matter? He's dead. And as far as I can tell, it's your fault."

"It might matter, Banks. I want to explain. I want to make this all right, but I didn't come here to win you back. I—"

"That's good to know, because I'm done with you, Chris. Or Reed. Or whoever the hell you are. You're just like every other deadbeat on the planet. Happy to get into my pants on a dark stormy night, and just as happy to leave me high and dry when shit hits the fan. Only you're worse because you're actually a horrible person."

As she spoke, her words faded from angry outbursts to weaker and weaker sobs. She finally broke off and slumped against the wall, her face turning red as sweat dripped down her cheeks.

"What's happening?" Reed asked. "Are you sick?"

"Of course I'm sick. Don't you know everything?"

"Okay, well, where are your meds? What do you need?"

Banks closed her eyes and breathed heavily. Her fingers trembled, and she continued sweating, even though the A/C was set on full blast.

"I ran out. This happens sometimes. It's a flare-up."

"What do you need? I'll get it."

She glowered. "You got a bottle of fever-crushing antibiotics in your back pocket?"

Reed unzipped his backpack, digging through it before tossing three different medicine bottles onto the damp blankets. "Take your pick."

Banks picked up the first bottle and read the label, then snorted. "My God. You really are a killer."

"I prefer to think of myself as an adult Boy Scout. Always prepared."

Banks shoved two pills into her mouth and washed them down with another gulp of water before slouching back on her pillow. Her skin, a constant alternation of flaming red and snow white, now faded into an irregular blotchy pattern of both.

Reed took the bottle back. "What does it do? The disease, I mean."

"It's an infection that comes from ticks. It can lay dormant for years, then ignite out of nowhere. Fevers, nausea, insomnia, aches, muscle spasms."

"Fainting?"

She licked her lips. "Sometimes."

"I'm sorry."

She glowered toward him. "*Never* say that to me again. I'm nobody's victim."

Reed nodded slowly.

The glare faded, and Banks turned her bloodshot eyes toward the ceiling. "You're not leaving, are you?"

Reed shook his head.

"Then what are you doing here?"

Reed folded his arms. The silence that hung between them felt heavier than a loaded Marine rucksack on an uphill run. His mouth went dry, and he clawed at the edges of his mind, searching for an answer.

Why am I here? Did I honestly expect her to run into my arms?

"I'm here to protect you. You're not safe. And I'm here to find the truth."

Once again, her eyes closed, and her breaths came in ragged bursts. He thought she had faded away, sinking into a labored sleep, or fainting again. But then her lips parted, and she spoke in a calm whisper. "The truth about *what*?"

Reed stared at his worn and battered hands, crisscrossed with dirt, scars, and healing wounds. He didn't feel any pain, only numbness, and he was at a loss for answers. Should he tell her? Could he tell her?

"You told me your father died in a car wreck."

She gritted her teeth. "What does that have to do with anything?"

"You said it was an accident."

Banks didn't answer.

"Your godfather. . . . I spoke to him about your father. In detail."

Banks's eyes opened, and a tear slipped out. She faced him, the rage melting away into unsheltered heartache. "Let me guess. He told you it wasn't an accident. He told you Daddy was killed."

Reed tilted his head. "You know?"

"Of course I know. He told everyone that story. He spent months investigating it, badgering the cops, then one day, six months after Daddy died, he just quit. Went quiet. The police finally convinced him, I guess. Daddy died from a drunk driver. I guess Uncle Mitch wanted deeper justice."

Reed touched the bed next to Banks. She made no move to take his hand but turned her gaze to the ceiling. Reed withdrew his hand and clenched it into a fist over his knee. Every part of him ached inside, commanding him to hold her, to comfort her. To somehow take away the hurricane in her heart that ripped her apart from the inside. But he couldn't. Not now. The only thing he could do was what he should've done from day one—tell her the truth.

"It's true, Banks."

She faced him. "What's true?"

"Everything. My name is Reed Montgomery, and I'm a professional assassin. I was hired to kill your godfather by an underground organization that I believe he was associated with. I kidnapped him in Atlanta because keeping him alive was my best bet of saving you. While I held him captive, Mitch demanded to know if I had killed your father. The last thing he told me before he died was about the fraternity where he met Frank."

"What are you saying?" she whispered.

"I'm saying your father was murdered by the same people who murdered Mitch. They also kidnapped you, sent the assassin after us in North Carolina, and murdered a very dear friend of mine. I'm here because I'm going to find them, whoever they are. I'm going to make them confess what they've done, and then I'm going to destroy them."

16

"I'm sorry, Madam Governor. We did everything we could."

Maggie nodded once. The doctor's footsteps faded, and for a brief moment, the clatter and chaos of the emergency room faded with them.

Dan touched her arm. "Maggie, I'm sorry. We have to address the media."

Ah, yes. The media, already clustered around the sliding doors at the entrance of the ER, ready to descend upon their governor with all the wrath and ferocity of a herd of vultures. It wasn't that she hated the media or was unappreciative of their role in society; she simply resented their callousness. No matter the tragedy, the loss, or the heartache of the situation, the only thing a reporter cared about was the headline. That sort of detached mission-focus was the heart of Louisiana's problems. People forgot about people.

"Fine," she said. "Assemble them outside. I'll freshen up."

The bathroom at the end of the hall featured a small, dirty mirror and a counter that Maggie was afraid to touch. She brushed her hair back behind her ears and held it in place with a hairband, then refreshed her makeup and lipstick. A brief survey in the mirror left her satisfied she'd avoid any media gaffs about her appearance, and she turned to the door.

A crowd of TV and newspaper reporters was already knotted around the door, jostling each other for position as Dan called for them to calm down and wait for Maggie. He was good at that, Maggie thought. Dan was never designed to be an executive, but he absolutely thrived as a lieutenant governor. He understood people, understood how to get the sludge moving, and most importantly, he could tell the difference between overstepping his own authority and bothering Maggie with things he could manage on his own.

Maggie straightened the collar of her blouse and checked her reflection one more time in the sliding glass door, then straightened her back and stepped out in front of the flashing lights.

The questions started immediately, but before Maggie could speak, Dan stepped forward and barked into the microphone. "Let me be perfectly clear. The next time we hold a press conference and questions are asked before the governor has an opportunity to make a statement, there will be *no* questions answered for that conference. Are we understood? Thank you."

Maggie nodded her thanks at Dan, then approached the middle of the crowd. Several microphones were held out toward her, and she offered a polite smile. "Thank you all for coming out on such short notice. It is with tremendous sadness that I announce that Officers Green and Maxwell, two lead members of my personal detail, passed away early this morning of wounds sustained while protecting me against an attempted assassination."

A low gasp rang out through the crowd. One or two reporters leaned forward, indicating an impending question, but Dan snapped his fingers, and the reporter fell back. Maggie accepted a bottle of water from Yolanda, took a long sip, and blinked away her exhaustion. It still hadn't registered that two of her own men were killed. It still didn't make sense that somebody had tried to take her life. It all felt detached, as though it were happening to somebody else.

"Officers Green and Maxwell were more than servants of the state. They were my friends. I knew the names of their kids, and they knew how I liked my coffee. They were good men—the finest the state of Louisiana has to offer, and their sacrifice is a debt we can never repay. Having said that, I have already outlined an initiative with the LSP to ensure that both officers' families are financially sustained for life out of honor for their sacrifice. Investigations as to the identity of the assassin are underway, and we have very limited information at this time. I will now take a few questions."

One hand shot up before she finished speaking, and Maggie resisted a sigh. "Yes, Ms. Simmons?"

"Can you comment on the policy in place within the LSP for death pensions of this type? I wasn't aware that the executive branch had the authority to grant cash disbursements on command."

The muscles in her back tensed, and Maggie consciously relaxed to avoid appearing combative. "Existing LSP compensation programs will be leveraged to ensure the financial security of the Green and Maxwell families. Any further compensation will be arranged as required because that's the right thing to do. Any other questions?"

"Madam Governor, can you comment as to why this attempted assassination took place so far from the Capitol, in an unsecured rural area near Lake Maurepas?"

Maggie shot Dan a sideways look. He shook his head, and she turned back to the crowd.

"Details of the circumstance surrounding the attempted assassination will not be disclosed at this time to protect the integrity of the investigation."

"Madam Governor, don't you think the people will find it strange that our female governor was inexplicably absent from the Capitol, attended only by her two male guards?"

Blood and a growing rage surged into Maggie's skull. Before answering, she waited five seconds, staring directly into the reporter's eyes. "The Executive Office is under no obligation to report on the travel agenda or accommodations of the governor, and the people of Louisiana will have to content themselves with the public results of the investigation as soon as they are available. Thank you, everyone. That will be all."

Maggie turned away from the mics as questions continued to rise from the small crowd of reporters. Dan stepped in behind her and made a brief statement regarding the governor's gratitude to the press, then followed her across the parking lot to a jet-black Tahoe waiting for them. Maggie piled inside and slammed the door, resting her head in her hands. The exhaustion of the last twenty-four hours descended on her full force, making it difficult to think clearly.

"How did they know?" she demanded.

Dan buckled his seatbelt and leaned back, taking a deep breath before answering. "I don't know, Maggie. Somebody must have leaked it."

Maggie dug her fingers into the leather seat as the big engine rumbled and the Tahoe turned toward the Capitol.

"Dan, you *know* why I was at the lake house. It's disgusting that they would insinuate anything scandalous when two of my men are *dead*!" The end of her sentence cracked, and she leaned forward into her hands again, rubbing both temples.

"I agree with you, Maggie, but your parting shots only added fuel to that fire. They're journalists. This is what they do."

"That was *not* journalism," Maggie snapped. "That was fishing for tabloid gossip."

Dan handed her a bottle of water and waited for her to take a sip before replying. "Again, I agree. But you have to be very careful not to come across too aggressively. It will hurt you more than it helps. They're only looking for drama, and the way you manage that is by feeding them the drama *you* want to be proliferated. Do you understand? You have to play this smart."

Maggie stared out the window, watching the city streets and stoplights flash by. The exhaustion she felt in her soul was deeper than just a lack of sleep. It was true, total frustration with every aspect of her life.

"This is exactly why I hate politics," she muttered.

Dan grunted. "Yep. And it's exactly why the state needs you now more than ever. You're here to bring Baton Rouge back from the depths. But these things take time, and you have to work with what you have. That includes the media."

Maggie stared through the glass. Dan's ability to view things objectively was the counterbalance of her fire-and-brimstone approach to destroying corruption, and she knew she needed that. She knew she needed to listen.

But dammit, she was still pissed.

"Have you heard back from Jackson?"

Dan sighed. "Yes, I got an email an hour ago."

"And?"

"They confirmed the presence of poison. It'll take a day or two for the autopsy to confirm the exact type and amount, but we can now safely assume Attorney General Matthews died of unnatural means."

"So, he *was* assassinated."

"It looks that way. Again, we'll need more time to formulate an official report."

"That's fine. Where are you with the special election?"

"We can announce dates next week. My recommendation is to hold the general election no sooner than eight months from now, to give time for the primaries. I know you want to rush it, but—"

"No, I agree. Eight months is fine. What about an intermediary?"

Dan lifted his briefcase off the floor and clicked it open. "You'll need to appoint an acting attorney general—somebody to hold office until after the special election. I've already assembled a list of suggestions that—"

"Robert Coulier."

The SUV fell deathly quiet as Maggie rubbed her bottom lip.

Dan shut the briefcase. "Is that a *joke*?"

"Do I sound like I'm joking?"

"Maggie, he's been *disbarred*. He doesn't even live here!"

"He's been disbarred in Texas. His law license is still active in Louisiana. He maintains an address in Shreveport and has for more than five years. That makes him a resident, and qualifies him for the office."

"Maggie, look at me, please."

She took another sip of water and faced Dan. The fear in his eyes was that of a person who's been pushed too far out of his comfort zone. She had seen that look several times before. Dan never liked to play the wild cards.

Then again, Dan wasn't the governor.

"You can't put a man like that in office."

"Actually, I can. I'm governor. You said so yourself."

Dan laid both hands over his knees and wrapped his fingers into his cotton slacks. "What I mean is, if you do this, the media will have a feeding frenzy. It'll be open season on your every move. The critics will go wild. You could easily lose the faith of the public—"

"The public elected me less than a year ago. They elected me to do a job —to lead this state and destroy corruption. That's what I'm going to do. The worst that could happen is they don't reelect me. In the meantime, I need somebody in the AG's office with teeth. I have no guarantee who will be elected to fill that spot, or how spineless they may be. That means I have eight months to get as much done as possible, and I need a pit bull to make it happen. Coulier is a pit bull if ever I met one."

"You're right, and that's why he was disbarred. He pushes too hard. Gets too aggressive. You put a man like that in the Capitol, and you'll have every corrupt politician, aid, lobbyist, and pundit turned against you overnight. They'll panic. They'll band together."

A faint smile played at the corners of Maggie's mouth. "That's exactly what we want. Set up a meeting with Coulier."

17

"I should gut you."

Reed sat with his hands in his lap, watching as Banks slurped down mouthfuls of chicken noodle soup. "That's a fair sentiment."

Banks scooped up another puny chunk of chicken and gulped it down, then leaned back and surveyed him through tired eyes. "What the hell happened to your throat?"

Reed touched his neck. He hadn't taken a look in the mirror since the incident in Chattanooga, but he imagined the skin to be purple by now. Every breath and swallow hurt like hell, only mildly subdued by the Tylenol pills he took earlier that day. "That guy from the mountains. Bumped into him again."

Banks grunted. "Pity he didn't finish the job."

The words stung, leaving Reed wondering if she felt any of the confused, twisted emotions that he had battled since they first met. Did she ache, longing for the way things had felt before? Or did she simply hate him beyond words?

"I'm sure he'll be back. Maybe you'll get your wish."

"Maybe I'll help him." Her tone was cold.

"Don't you want to know?" Reed asked. "Don't you want the truth about what happened to your father?"

Banks lingered over her bowl, staring into the yellow depths of the broth and poking at the noodles with her spoon. "What if I do?"

"That's something I can help with."

She glared at him.

"Banks, I'm not trying to win you back. I know I'm a horrible person. But there are people out there who are worse than me. They killed Mitch, and I believe they killed your father. I want revenge . . . for your people and mine."

"What was her name?" Banks spat the question.

"I'm sorry?"

"Your friend. It was a *she*, right? Another woman?"

"It wasn't like that."

"Don't bullshit me, dammit. What was her name?"

Reed averted his eyes. "Kelly."

Banks tipped the bowl up and sucked down the broth, then wiped her mouth with the back of her hand. "Did you love her?"

Reed thought back to the last time he saw Kelly standing by her kitchen counter, just the hint of a baby belly building beneath her shirt. She looked different than she had in Monaco—less fit, a lot less wild. She wasn't the girl who rescued him from the French police, but she resembled her.

"Yes," he said. "I loved her. A long time ago."

"Isn't that nice? Guess that didn't work out for her, either."

Reed gritted his teeth and stood up. "I'm sorry, Banks. I lied to you, I hurt you, and I hurt those closest to you. I'm a despicable, deplorable human being. There's nothing more I can say. I came here because I felt like you deserved the truth and an apology. I'll go now. Good luck with everything."

Reed started for the door, his own words echoing in his ears, ripping deeper than hers had.

"If what you say is true, those people are still alive. The people who killed my father."

Reed stopped and put his hands in his pockets. "Yes."

Banks stood up, and he turned to see her bright blue eyes blazing fire toward him.

"Then you're not going anywhere until you bring me justice. Am I clear?"

Reed nodded slowly. "Okay."

"Great. I'm going to change. I hope you know where to start."

He didn't hesitate. "Vanderbilt University. We're starting at the beginning."

"What the hell is this thing?"

Banks stood back from the Camaro, her arms crossed as she glared down at the car. She wore a loose Guns N' Roses T-shirt that fell over one shoulder, with torn-out jeans and tennis shoes. The color had balanced in her face, but he could still detect the effort it took for her to make every step.

"Camaro Z/28. Slightly modified."

"You drive it like you drove my Beetle?"

"It's a little faster than your Beetle."

"A little less destroyed, too."

Reed chose to ignore the comment and unlocked the driver's door. He leaned the seat forward and whistled softly. "Come out, boy."

Baxter lumbered out of the back seat. With each step, he grunted as his scalded skin rippled over his body.

"Oh my God," Banks cried. She rushed around the car and knelt in front of the bulldog. "You poor baby. What happened to you?"

Baxter tilted his head back, peering at Banks. She touched his head, stroking behind his ears as she examined the burn marks and singed skin.

"He's a rescue," Reed said. "He was in a house fire."

"You poor thing." Banks ran gentle fingers over his back and kissed his head. Baxter shot Reed a sideways look, his eyes laden with smug satisfaction.

"Oh, shut up," Reed snorted.

"I'm taking him inside. He can't ride around in that thing anymore."

Banks tugged on Baxter's collar, speaking gently to the old dog as she led him up the sidewalk toward her apartment door. Baxter complied without complaint, his stubby tail twitching as Banks continued to stroke and console him with gentle words.

Reed slid into the driver seat and slammed the door. The motor coughed twice before its comforting purr filled the cabin.

Banks returned ten minutes later and plopped down in the passenger seat, shooting Reed another glare. "That puppy needs medicine, a decent diet, and a lot of rest. I don't know what you think you're doing, dragging him around in the back seat of a car."

Reed blinked. "Um . . . he's my dog . . ."

"We'll see about that, shithead. Now start driving. We've got work to do."

Reed slid the car out of the parking lot and back onto the street. To the southeast, the Nashville skyline rose above condominiums and shiny business centers. The Camaro roared through a small residential district before turning south toward Midtown.

West of downtown, Vanderbilt University, a booming medical and legal college, lay nestled amongst a crowd of restaurants, housing, and small businesses. Reed had encountered several graduates during his tenure as a professional killer, but he'd never laid foot on the university grounds.

"What's your plan, exactly?" Banks demanded. She looked out the window, watching passing buildings with her arms crossed.

Reed rolled to a stop at a light and fought to clear his tired mind. What *was* his plan? For some time now, his only objective had been to find Banks, then find the people who killed Kelly. After gunning down Cedric Muri, he wasn't entirely sure where to look next.

"Your godfather attended Vanderbilt the same time as your dad. They were both members of a fraternity, and Mitch indicated that things began—"

"What precisely did Uncle Mitch say about the fraternity?"

"Well . . ." Reed searched his memory, trying to recall every moment with Holiday as the senator lay dying on the lakeshore. "His exact words were, '*From end to end.*'"

"'From end to end?' What the hell does that have to do with a frat?"

"I found a picture of him standing beside your father at a ceremony. The name of the fraternity was written on the back. *Omega, Alpha, Omega*— the last, first, and last letter of the Greek alphabet. From end to end."

"Seriously?" Banks rolled her eyes. "*That's* what led you to Vanderbilt? That could mean anything, shithead."

"You know, I liked *cowboy* a lot better than *shithead.*"

"Well, I liked Chris a lot better than Reed. Shame we can't have what we like."

Reed dug his fingers into the Alcantara covering of the steering wheel, biting back the urge to retaliate, and refocusing on the task at hand. "We're going to find the frat house for Omega Alpha Omega and check the membership records. Find any photographs or meeting minutes we can. There had to be other members besides Mitch and Frank who can give us a clue where to look next."

Banks said nothing.

She's devastated. She's either aching inside or she hates me, but it's no more than I deserve.

Reed navigated the car off of West End Avenue and through the main entrance of the university. Large metal signs advertised Vanderbilt's founding in 1873. Trees, barren of leaves, overhung the parking lot, sheltering a string of fancy foreign cars sitting in front of "reserved for faculty" signs.

Reed parked at the back of the lot under a magnolia tree, then turned to Banks. "I get it. You hate me, and I can deal with that. But if we want to find what we're looking for, you have to work with me. Feuding like this isn't going to get us anywhere."

Banks rolled her eyes again. "Get your head out of your ass, shithead. I'll let you live a while longer."

She piled out of the car and slammed the door. Reed watched her go, then ran an exhausted hand over his face.

Here goes nothing.

18

The man that sat across the desk from Maggie was neither handsome nor homely. He wore a brown suit—yes, the man actually wore a brown suit—and a soft yellow shirt, unbuttoned halfway down with no tie. Bald, with a dusting of hair just above his ears, and a wiry goatee that matched his shirt. In spite of his frumpy appearance, his teeth were impeccably straight and white, his eyes sharp and bright, and his posture stiff. He had the look of a man who knew his worth and didn't give a crap if anyone else did or not.

Maggie leaned back in her chair and tried to appear casual. In spite of her title, she felt a shadow of intimidation sitting across from Robert Coulier. The man had a reputation in the greater Texarkana area—a ruthless, brutal, cold-blooded lawyer with absolutely no interest in cutting deals or taking prisoners. Disbarred in Texas for repeated witness intimidation, Coulier now practiced international law for Chinese businesses out of his Shreveport office, but he was never there. Known simply as "The Dog," he was feared by defense counsel and hated by legal academia as a brutish example of what law could become. Vile, profane, grizzly.

In spite of all this, Maggie had always respected Coulier. It wasn't because he always won, although that certainly didn't hurt. It was because he was true to himself. He knew what he wanted, he knew how to get it, and he didn't compromise.

The only wild card? Sometimes what he wanted conflicted with standard ethics. The Dog would need a leash.

"Mr. Coulier, I can't thank you enough for flying out on such short notice. I know you have a busy schedule."

Coulier nodded once but didn't reply. He folded his hands in his lap and stared Maggie down, unblinking.

Maggie gestured to the decanter sitting on the end table nearby. "Can I get you a beverage?"

Coulier smiled. "I don't drink, Madam Governor. It disrupts my sleep patterns."

"Of course." Maggie offered a warm smile. "I hear you keep long hours. They say you barely sleep at all."

"I sleep for three hours every ten. This enables me to be the most productive."

"That's something we have in common. I usually sleep only a few hours a night, although I'm afraid it's not as regular as I'd like. The burden of the office, I guess. Do you use sleep aids?"

Coulier's smile remained plastered to his face, neither friendly nor cold. All business.

"Madam Governor, I appreciate your eloquence, but neither one of us have the time. Why am I here?"

Maggie placed her hands on the table, palms down. Her body language advisor told her this gesture displayed confidence and authority. It felt awkward.

"Right. Of course. Well, as I'm sure you know, we've recently lost out attorney general. The official statement is that the investigation is ongoing, but confidentially I can tell you his death was not an accident. We're pursuing a homicide investigation now."

Coulier didn't comment. Maggie shifted her hands on the desktop, then cleared her throat.

"As governor, it's my responsibility to appoint an interim AG until a special election can be held. I'm currently reviewing candidates, and—"

"I'll do it." Coulier's tone remained calm but confident. Maggie raised her eyebrows.

"I didn't offer you the job."

"You flew me from Beijing on taxpayer dollars, and we both know you don't have any other candidates. The only reason I came is because I want the job."

Maggie sat back in her chair and folded her arms. She wasn't entirely sure how to respond. On the one hand, his confidence and directness were exactly the reasons she wanted him in the first place. On the other, she wanted to ask him herself. She needed him to obey and respect her authority. This wasn't a great start.

"Why do you want the job?"

Coulier relaxed his shoulders and crossed his legs. "Why does anyone want to be the lead legal officer of a state? Power. Prestige. Influence. Access."

Maggie smirked. "I appreciate your eloquence, but neither of us has the time. Why do you really want it?"

This time Coulier's smile was genuine. He tilted his head and stared at her for a full minute, as though he were evaluating an expensive piece of art he was contemplating purchasing. She didn't blink and stared right back, arms still crossed.

"I'm sure you're aware that I'm not an altogether popular attorney," he said.

"I am."

"I'm sure you know why."

"I do."

"Only one thing makes me tick, Madam Governor. *Winning.* I live for the win. I breathe for it. Winning is in my blood. I don't care about money, fame, or renown. I just want to conquer. Five years ago, I was engaged in litigation against a large oil firm that operates off the Louisiana coast. The case started as a single-plaintiff lawsuit about unsafe work environments on their oil platforms. One of their welders lost his leg to a falling piece of steel, and he wanted compensation. Seemed like a home run case to me, so I took it. But as soon as I began litigation, everything spilled over. I found thousands of cases of muted OSHA filings, wrongfully denied workman's comp claims, workers who were fired for reporting unsafe working conditions, bribes paid to regulators, and every other type of corporate corruption. So, I advised my client to allow me to pursue a class-action lawsuit and involve other plaintiffs. I didn't see how I could lose."

"But you did."

Coulier's smile faded. "You're very astute. I was sabotaged. The defense delayed and dragged their feet every possible way they could. They insisted on a trial, and stacked the jury, all while launching a slander campaign against me for my difficulties in Texas. I fought to the end, but I lost. Not a single dollar was paid out to my clients, and no regulatory measures were improved. Ryman Offshore Partners continues unmitigated operations to this day."

Maggie lifted a glass of water from the executive desk and took a sip. Coulier waited, his expression impassive and unreadable.

"So," she said. "Now you want revenge."

"No, Madam Governor. Like I told you before, there is only one thing I want. I want to win. In this case, winning means destroying Ryman. And when I'm finished with them, I will win with the state judge who presided over the case, who refused the admission of key evidence and sheltered the jury. Then I will win over the defense counsel."

"Double jeopardy law prevents you from trying them for any of the regulatory infractions they've already been acquitted of," Maggie said.

"I won't need to. Dirty hands are seldom soiled with a single variety of mud. Trust me when I tell you, Governor, I've been collecting ammunition against my enemies from the day the ruling was issued. All guilty parties will be charged within two days of my inauguration."

Maggie laid her hands on the desk again and stared Coulier down. She tried to imagine what was happening behind that impassive stare and blunt honesty. She didn't think he was lying or would have a reason to lie, and she appreciated his absolute candor. This was exactly the sort of agenda-driven bloodthirst Coulier was known for, and she could only imagine the meltdown Dan would descend into if he were sitting in the room with them. Obviously, that was why Dan wasn't invited to attend the interview. She anticipated Coulier would have some type of personal agenda from the moment he readily accepted her invitation to the Capitol. Granted, this was a bit more extreme than she had hoped for. Somehow, it still didn't alarm her.

"Well, I appreciate your bluntness," she said. "Do you know what *I* want?"

The smile returned to Coulier's thin lips. "You want to fulfill your campaign promises. You want to destroy political and corporate corruption."

Maggie returned the smile. "Yes, sir. I very much do, and I need a pit bull to make that happen. They tell me you're a dog. Can you be a dog who hunts more than one raccoon?"

The smile spread into an unabashed grin, fully exposing the flawless white teeth. "Governor, I was born to hunt."

Maggie stood up and offered her hand. "Welcome to Baton Rouge, Mr. Attorney General."

19

Reed didn't have a great deal of experience with college campuses, but he guessed that most of them weren't as pretty as Vanderbilt—a fusion of old trees and older brick buildings, with sidewalks that wound between them like hidden paths in a magic forest. Students bustled back and forth across the streets, burdened down with backpacks and laptop cases. Some were teenagers, but many were much older.

They found their way to the student information hall, and Banks stopped Reed at the foot of the steps. "You're gonna need to look less like a killer, or the police will be here in no time."

"What do you mean? I look fine."

Banks rolled her eyes and ran her hand through his hair, ruffling it up before she yanked at his shirt, untucking it. "I'm not going down for your sins, you fool."

Fool is better than shithead.

She turned and started up the steps. "All right, shithead. Be cool."

Annnnnnnd we're back.

The big brick building at the top of the steps featured dual glass doors guarded by a concrete arch. Inside, small clusters of students gathered around desks with old, tired counselors seated behind. Must hung in the air, as though many of the books were far older than the librarians who kept them and would likely sit on these shelves long after their guardians had passed on.

Reed slouched his shoulders and leaned forward, trying to imagine what a college student looked like. The young males around him were as diverse as a promotional billboard. Some wore ties and button-down shirts, with slicked-back hair and rimless glasses. Others appeared more relaxed —sports T-shirts and tennis shoes.

"Can I help you?" The overweight woman behind the counter sounded as though she were interested in doing anything but. Even so, she offered them a polite smile as they approached.

"My brother is looking for information on fraternities." Banks smiled so sweetly, Reed felt his heart skip. He looked away and feigned interest over a poster on the wall.

The old woman grumbled. "Rush week is over. I can give you a list of on-campus organizations, though." She rustled through her drawer and produced a glossy brochure with a group of smiling kids wearing back-packs. She passed it across the counter, and Reed scooped it up. A quick scan of the names and addresses listed under the *"fraternities"* tab came up emptyhanded.

"What about Omega Alpha Omega?" he asked.

"I'm sorry?"

"I don't see them on the list."

She shook her head. "I've never heard of Omega Alpha Omega. Every Vanderbilt fraternity is on that list. You must have the name wrong."

Reed scanned the list again. Many names he recognized from years of reading assassination profiles, as some of his more professional targets were frat members. But Omega Alpha Omega wasn't on the list.

"Is there something else I can help with?" The impatience in her tone was evident. Reed shook his head and turned toward the door, leaving Banks to offer a quick thank-you before scuttling after him. The cold air outside the building flooded his lungs, bringing welcome relief from the stuffiness of the student hall. Once more, he scanned the brochure, but it was pointless. Holiday's old fraternity wasn't there.

"What now?" Banks snapped. "Did you get the name wrong?"

"No, I definitely had it right. The letters were very clear."

"Where's the picture?"

Reed tapped the edge of the brochure against his lip and pretended not to have heard her.

Banks pinched his arm. "Don't fool around with me. Where's the picture?"

He sighed and dug out his wallet, producing the faded photograph of Mitch Holiday and Frank Morccelli in fraternity robes. Banks snatched it away and fixated on the image. Her eyes turned red before she flipped it over and read the back.

"See? Omega Alpha Omega," Reed said. "I had the name right. And that *does say* Vanderbilt University."

Banks tapped the photo against her fingers. Confused emotions clouded her face, and Reed guessed it had little to do with the location of the mystery fraternity.

"Let's head over to the row and take a look around," she said.

"The *row?*"

Banks rolled her eyes. "Wow, you really are a moron. The row—where all the frat and sorority houses are. Every campus has one. Look at the addresses."

Reed scanned the brochure again, and sure enough, several of the head-quarters' addresses were on the same street. The pamphlet's map guided them through a series of tree-sheltered sidewalks deeper inside the campus.

In spite of the bustle of students, everything was calm. Reed wondered what it must feel like to be one of them—jogging to their next class, the most stressful thing in the world their latest grade or midterm. In times past, he hated people like them. As a gangbanger in Los Angeles, he viewed all college kids as rich, spoiled brats who wasted their lives away with their noses crammed into books.

Now, things weren't so black and white. Jealousy tugged within him, and he wondered what his life could have been like if he'd never joined the gangs, never ran into the recruiter, and never became a Marine. Would he have gone to college? Probably not a school like Vanderbilt—who was he kidding?—but maybe a state school. He could've studied something like business or marketing, worked in a tall, glassy tower like the ones in downtown Nashville, dated a nice girl, and had a couple kids.

"What's wrong with you?" Banks's snapping voice jarred him out of the daydream. He realized he had stopped on the sidewalk, his gaze transfixed by the crowds of students bustling by. Everything about his picture of another life, for another Reed, felt surreal and frail, built on a foundation of false realities that could never have come to pass.

I wasn't born to be like them. I was born for something different. Something hard.

"Let's move, dumbass."

"Look." Reed withdrew his hands from his pockets and folded his arms. "If you want to know the truth about what happened to your father, I'm the best way. I'm not asking you to like me, but I'm not your enemy."

"Not my enemy?" Banks wheeled on him and stepped so close he could smell her breath laden with tequila, even though he hadn't seen her take a drink since he found her at the bar. She jabbed a finger into his chest. "You *lied* to me—about everything. You kidnapped my uncle, brutalized him, and swept me up in this entire mess. I almost died *twice* because of you. If you're not my enemy, I don't know who is."

The fire that blazed in her eyes was every bit as bright and fierce as it had been the first night he met her, but these flames didn't speak of joy and ambition and a passionate hunger for life. This time, the dark embers smoldered with resentment.

"I understand that. Believe me. I hate myself more than you hate me. And when this is over, if you want to push me off a cliff, that's fine. But right now, we have a chance to discover the truth, and I have a chance to punish the people responsible. *They* are the enemy. If you want to do it on your own, be my guest, but if you can find it in your heart to suspend your hatred for just a few days, I can help you. I want to help you."

She stared him down, her finger still pressed into his chest. He thought she might slap him, but she turned away. "Fine. Help me. But this doesn't mean I've forgiven or forgotten."

They started down the sidewalk again, watching trees fade into small parks and brick buildings into old homes. Flags hung from the columns of front porches, displaying the proud symbols of a half dozen sororities and fraternities. A few homes featured Greek letters over the front doors, while a handful of kids shuffled in and out, backpacks over their shoulders, evidence of hangovers in their sloppy steps.

None of the signs or flags matched Omega Alpha Omega. Reed and Banks walked down the street, then turned back on the other side, stopping from time to time to ask passing students if they had heard of the fraternity. Blank stares and shrugs were the most expressive responses they received, except for one shirtless frat boy, still drunk, who grinned and invited them inside.

Banks leaned against a tree and pushed her hands into her jean pockets. Her face was flushed red again, and in spite of the breeze, sweat trickled down her neck.

Reed moved toward her. "Are you okay?"

She jutted her chin toward the street. "It's not here. This frat of yours doesn't exist."

"You saw the letters," Reed said. "It exists. Or at least it did at some point. Maybe they didn't have a frat house, and they met in the library or off campus."

"So how do we find them? It's a big city."

Reed looked back down the narrow street, his eyes coming to rest on a house three doors down that featured a blue flag with gold letters. The two-story house was white with strips of peeling paint hanging from the siding. Big windows framed the second floor, and a small skylight overhung what must have been the attic. Dead grass around the home was sheltered by untrimmed evergreen bushes, and compared to the surrounding rows of manicured homes with clean yards, the house stood out like a sore thumb. A small crowd of college kids were busy unloading a van, carting food and cases of beer into the house.

"What do you suppose they're doing?" Reed asked.

Banks shrugged. "What all frat boys do. Partying, or getting ready for a party."

"Yeah, I know, but look at the house. It's a shamble."

"So they don't take care of it. What's your point?"

Reed started down the street, walking along the curb as he surveyed the home. The paint clinging to the walls had peeled and dropped into the grass in sheets—everywhere except the fascia over the front porch. A towering oak tree sheltered the home, where the frat's three-letter name was mounted in gold letters. Each letter was clean, with fresh paint and not a speck of dirt—a sharp contrast to the wall they were mounted against.

The letters are new.

Banks stumbled to a stop beside him, peered at the house, then shook her head. "I don't get it."

Reed held up his finger as the clouds began to part. A sunray cut through the oak tree's ragged limbs and spilled over the fascia. The bright light exposed the shadowy outline of a sign: Omega, Alpha, Omega. It was hung long before on that same facade, protecting the paint beneath it from the scar of the sun, and leaving its outline, even after it was torn down.

Reed turned to Banks, and a slow smile spread across her face, spilling into her eyes for the first time since she took the stage at the bar earlier that day.

"They're taking over the house," she said. "It's been abandoned."

"Yes. For God knows how long. Those letters were probably pirated for use on another house years ago, which explains why nobody knew it was the old Omega Alpha Omega headquarters."

"We've got to get inside. There could be old records. Logbooks. Information on who else was in the fraternity that might still be alive."

Reed started across the street, slumping his shoulders and trying to appear as casual as possible as he approached the kids unloading the van. "'Sup, guys? Need a hand?"

An underage redheaded teen took a sip of beer and poked his head around the back door of the van. He surveyed Reed with squinted eyes, then his gaze traveled to Banks. His demeanor shifted. "You guys students?"

Banks nodded and offered her hand. "Yeah, I'm Sirena. We're from Iowa."

"No shit!" He grinned and shook her hand. "So am I! What city?"

She had to pick Iowa.

"Iowa City. Born and raised. You guys prepping for a party?"

His grin widened, and Reed checked his first assumption when he noticed the black-and-yellow Hawkeyes baseball hat hanging on the van's rearview mirror.

She's a manipulative genius.

The frat boy ran his hand through his short red hair. "You bet. Gonna throw a little celebration party tonight. We just got a lease on this place. Dope, right?"

Banks pretended to be impressed with the shabby building, leaning back and tilting her head up.

"Looks great, man! Sounds like fun."

He nodded, still staring at her curvy body, then blinked as though his mind had come awake. "Hey, you guys should come! It's gonna be rad. Got a DJ and everything."

Banks shot Reed a smug smirk, then directed a grin back at the kid. "What time?"

"We're kicking off at eight. Bring booze!"

Banks gave him a fist bump. As they walked back onto the street, Reed caught sight of a new wave of sweat dripping down her face, now faded from red to white.

She's barely standing.

"We should go back to your place. You need to rest. Then we can hit them up tonight."

"Oh, what a master plan. Come up with that all on your own, did you?"

Reed wanted to cringe but rolled his eyes. "Fine. *Thank you, you manipulative genius.* Your skills of sexual mind control are unmatched."

Banks turned off the street, back toward the Camaro. "You haven't seen anything yet."

20

Baton Rouge, Louisiana

The restaurant was quaint, dressed in white trim, and built inside an antebellum home with a wraparound porch now converted into an outdoor dining space. Maggie might have been impressed under different circumstances. Even excited. Instead, she surveyed the crowd of people sitting under whining ceiling fans on the porch and wondered if they were witnesses or potential victims.

On one side of her Tahoe, two men stood stiff-backed, surveying the downtown streets of Baton Rouge. She turned to a black-suited state policeman standing at attention next to her vehicle. "What's your name?" she asked.

"Officer O'Dell, Madam Governor." He spoke with a Cajun accent so thick and oppressive it was difficult even for her to discern the exact words.

She rested one hand on her hip. "Is that what your parents call you?"

Confusion flashed behind his eyes, and he shook his head. "No, ma'am. My first name is James."

"That's a great name, James. My first name is Maggie. We'll be spending a lot of time together from now on, so let's drop the formalities. Is that okay?"

Discomfort radiated from O'Dell's stiff shoulders and rigid arms like heat waves of a Louisiana bayou, but he nodded. "Yes, ma'am. If you prefer so, ma'am."

"I do. Now, James, I'm going to get a bite to eat. I want you to stay with the Tahoe. I'll be back shortly."

"Madam Governor, I'm afraid I can't allow that. I have to accompany you at all times."

Maggie raised an eyebrow. "Did your commanding officer tell you that?"

"Yes, ma'am."

"And who do you think he reports to? Don't worry, James. I can look after myself. Keep the motor running. I won't be long." Maggie stepped away from the vehicle and walked up the short row of white concrete steps.

A hostess greeted her at the front door, taking a small bow and motioning her toward the door. "Just one tonight, ma'am?"

"No, I'm meeting somebody. A gentleman."

"Yes, of course, ma'am. He mentioned you would be coming. Right this way."

The hostess led Maggie through a maze of chairs and tables, toward a small alcove in the rear. Full-length windows filled the whole wall, looking out over downtown Baton Rouge from the gentle hill the restaurant sat on.

A tall man in a grey suit sipped tea from a white cup as Maggie approached. He set the cup down at his table and offered his hand without standing. "Madam Governor, thank you so much for accepting my invitation."

Maggie ignored the hand and pulled back her chair, sitting without a word.

He tilted his head and smirked at her, then retracted his arm and lifted the cup again. "Would you care for something to drink? Dinner's on me."

"No, thank you. I won't be staying for dinner. I'm here because two of my men are dead, and you reached out to my office anonymously almost immediately after. Kind of strange, don't you think?"

The smirk remained plastered on his face. He stirred his tea with a silver spoon as the waitress approached.

"Ma'am, can I take your drink order?"

"Water," Maggie said. "Thank you."

The waitress retreated, and the man in the grey suit leaned forward, his lips turning down into a soft frown. "May I express my deepest condolences about your men. I read about the incident in the news this morning. What a tragic accident."

"Accident? Is that what they're calling it? News to me. You see, I was there. I saw the intruder. Shot him, as a matter of fact. Regrettably, he survived."

The smirk returned, and the man adjusted the teacup on its saucer.

"Maggie—may I call you Maggie?"

"You may not. I'm the governor."

"Yes, of course. Forgive me. Madam Governor, my name is Gambit. Well, that's not my actual name, but since you prefer titles, I suppose you can use mine."

"Gambit, I'm on a tight schedule. I've got a shitload of corruption to burn out of this state. I suggest you find your point."

"You're even saucier in person than you are on TV, Madam Governor. It's a true wonder anyone ever voted for you."

"Oh, plenty of people voted for me. Over six hundred thousand. It just so happens none of them were scumbags."

Gambit sat back. "Well, then, if you're going to be so curt, I may as well cut to the chase."

"You really should."

He sipped his tea, then cleared his throat. "I represent a *significant* organization of tremendous influence that would very much appreciate your partnership."

Maggie folded her hands. "So, you're a criminal, and you're here to enlist me in your elicit enterprises."

Gambit chuckled. "No, ma'am. As you said yourself, you're the governor of Louisiana. I wouldn't dream of involving you in anything less than legal. What my company proposes is more *mutually advantageous*. We simply want to count you as an ally. On occasion, we may ask you to redirect an investigation or help us with the approval of a permit. Perhaps offer us regulatory assistance. In exchange, we will ensure that whatever political initiatives you may have are completely successful—schools, roads, state parks . . . whatever you care about. We have the power to ensure you never lose an election. You can be governor for two terms, and then we might find you a home in the Senate. Who knows?" He took another sip of tea.

Maggie placed both hands on the table. "Well, Gambit, I believe this meeting is concluded. I'm afraid you have drastically miscalculated what type of person I am. I ran for the governorship to make a statement. I didn't even plan on winning. But I did win—and the reason I won is because scum like you have no place in this state, and the people of Louisiana want me to run you out. If you think for a moment that I'm going to have any part in whatever sordid activities you represent, you've got another thought coming. My *political initiatives* are to destroy people like you."

She stood up, and Gambit's smile faded. He stirred the tea again, then shook his head. "That's tragically unfortunate, Governor Trousdale. I always prefer honey, but I'm no stranger to vinegar. I understand you have a family who lives in the swamps outside New Orleans. I'm sure they're very important to you."

Maggie tilted her head and stared Gambit down. "My father can barely read, but he can hit a running rabbit at two hundred yards with a fifty-dollar rifle. My brother never finished high school, but he hunts gators for a living. My sister is a three-time national champion mixed martial artist. And my mom? The house was broken into last year, and she beat the burglar with a rolling pin. To my knowledge, he's still in a coma. If you'd like to threaten my family, Gambit . . . well, *good luck*."

Maggie walked past the oncoming waitress and back through the front door. O'Dell stood next to the Tahoe, his hand held close to the Glock .40 caliber mounted to his hip. He opened the door for Maggie, and she climbed in without comment. As the Tahoe pulled away, Gambit stood in the window, smiling at her. It was the smile of a man who enjoyed the hunt as much as he enjoyed the kill.

"James, I want protective details assigned to my family immediately. If the LSP gives you any flack about the cost, inform them that they can detract from my personal detail if necessary."

O'Dell nodded. "Yes, ma'am. Right away."

She folded her hands. "You know how to shoot that thing, or is it just a belt ornament?"

A smirk played at the corners of O'Dell's mouth, exposing the glint of a gold tooth in place of his lateral incisor. Their eyes met in the rearview mirror.

"Don't worry, ma'am. I know how to use it."

"Excellent." She closed her eyes and leaned back in her seat. "You just might have to."

21

Reed whistled as Banks slid into the Camaro wearing skintight jeans and a crop top. Her hair, heavily fragranced with perfume, hung over bare shoulders. Red lipstick coated her mouth, and dark eyeliner complemented heavy mascara.

Banks glared at him. "Keep it in your pants. This isn't for you."

He shifted into gear, and the Camaro rumbled away from Banks's apartment, back toward Vanderbilt. The city lay in darkness now, but it was far from asleep. Cars, Ubers, taxis, and every manner of modified-party contraption rolled down the streets, honking and shouting at every intersection. Reed felt his blood pressure rise as he fought his way through the mess, giving lower Broadway a wide berth before he turned west toward the campus.

Even before they could see the frat house, the thump of rap music filled their ears. Dull lights flashed into the sky in half a dozen neon colors, and students gathered around the front porch. Reed parked the Camaro fifty yards down the street and watched the house. In a crowd this dense, it would be next to impossible to conduct a thorough search of the old home.

"We need a plan," he said.

Banks sighed and opened her door. "How about this? I flash the frat kids, you find what we need."

Well, that seems workable.

Reed checked the SIG handgun tucked into his belt before joining Banks on the sidewalk. He could tell by her soft, labored breaths that she still felt terrible, but it didn't hold her back for a moment. Her hips swung gracefully as she trotted in heels toward the house. He couldn't help but admire her gentle strut, confident and calm, completely masking the clutch of illness on her body. His mind faded back to the two of them standing on the parking deck outside Atlanta, gazing at the skyline, while Banks strummed her ukulele. She was happier then, but no less a rock.

I want her back. God help me, I do.

A tall frat boy with broad shoulders and a drunken glare stumbled at the bottom of the steps. "Hey, this is a pwivate pawty."

Banks shot him a seductive smile and tilted her head, but it wasn't necessary. The redhead reappeared from the front door and waved his hand. "Don't worry, Max. I invited them. Wassup, baby?"

He winked at Banks, and she batted her eyelashes.

My God. How does somebody this idiotic get accepted at Vanderbilt?

Reed followed Banks up the steps and into the house. The beat of the music pounded inside his head, jarring his shoulders and flooding his mind with new aches. He eagerly sucked down the cup of cheap beer that was pressed into his hand.

"Welcome, brother! How's it going?"

Reed smiled and gave the kid a thumbs-up. Banks was already lost on the dance floor, swaying under the neon lights with the redhead grinding against her side. Reed felt his muscles tense, and he reached for the gun before his mind regained control of his reflexes.

She's doing her job. Do yours.

He glanced around the living room, now so packed with kids he could barely distinguish the walls. The Greek letters of the new frat hung over the kitchen doorway, and pinned to the living room wall was a fraternity constitution. Reed pushed his way into the kitchen, where two guys smoked joints, and a third leaned against the wall, making out with a brunette.

Much like the living room, the walls were bare, and nothing but alcohol covered the counters.

Reed pushed past the cloud of marijuana smoke and into the next room. It was the dining room, empty except for more cases of beer and a few cartons of fried chicken. He grabbed a drumstick and tore into it as he stepped into the hallway. His stomach grumbled from neglect, and the cold, greasy food relaxed his nerves. A frat boy—clearly a freshman—leaned over the toilet in the hallway bathroom and puked into the bowl. Reed couldn't resist a small smile.

Gonna be a long four years for you, my friend.

Inside a hallway closet built beneath the stairwell were a couple coats on hooks. A thorough investigation of their pockets produced nothing but cigarettes and weed. Reed mounted the steps and ascended to the second floor, softening each footfall as he drew closer. The music still pounded below, masking his footsteps as he passed the first bedroom. Empty. Light spilled out from beneath the next door. He placed his hand on the knob and started to twist, then heard soft moans and cries of ecstasy from the other side. He sighed and released the knob.

There has to be something more. They couldn't have cleared the whole house.

A window at the end of the hallway opened out over the backyard, where tall weeds were trampled under the feet of a few dozen more college kids, all sipping beer and swaying to the beat of hip-hop music. As Reed watched them, he marveled at how happy they looked—so loose and carefree.

Why does this piss me off? Am I seriously jealous of frat kids?

Reed started back toward the stairwell, then stopped. He remembered standing outside the house and staring up at the windows. There were skylights in the roof.

The attic.

A few paces down the hallway, Reed caught sight of the attic door. It was more of a hatch, really, about the size of a large pizza box, framed in the ceiling just above the window but obscured by shadows and cobwebs.

Reed stuck the light between his teeth and stepped up onto the windowsill. He pressed up with one hand on the tile, and it lifted free from the remainder of the ceiling with a shower of drywall particles. Reed shoved it aside and forced his head through the hole. Pine rafters and dust filled the space beyond, illuminated by the moonlight spilling through the skylights. He stuck both arms through the hole, then hauled himself above the ceiling. Flooring covered the upper side of the ceiling, providing a firm landing place as he rolled away from the hole.

Reed pulled himself to his feet and leaned against a rafter as his eyes scanned the plywood floor scattered with splotches of dark red. The residue was unmistakable. It was blood. Next to the blotches, systematic rows of dents in the wood lay in long, evenly spaced impressions. Chair legs?

Reed scanned the light around the room, hoping for an abandoned piece of paraphernalia from the vanishing fraternity, but found only dirt, dried blood, and shadows.

What the hell is this place?

Reed took another tentative step toward the end of the room. A board creaked under his foot, and he squinted at the far wall. It was different than the sloped roof that hugged his shoulders on either side. It was darker and softer looking, as if it wasn't built of wood at all.

Reed touched the black surface of the wall, covered floor to ceiling in dark cloth, confirming his suspicions. He wrapped his fingers into the fabric and jerked down. The breath rushed from his lips as the sheet fell, exposing the complete wall behind. Inches away, a large dark face stared directly into his. Reed leaped back and jerked the pistol from his hip, even as his mind recognized painted features on the wall.

It was the silver owl—the same one he had seen in the picture of Mitch Holiday and Frank Morccelli. Its blood-red eyes glared at Reed with all the malice and rage a painting could express. Reed slowly lowered the gun, then shuffled forward and reached out his hand, tracing the painted outlines whittled into the blackened plywood. The eyes weren't actually painted. They were glass, flat-backed, and glued to the wall. Reed traced the owl with the flashlight beam, moving all the way to the floor where the LED light exposed a wide pool of dried blood.

This was no fraternity.

Reed traced the edges of the wall, searching for any hidden passage or retractable piece of plywood, but the entire wall was fit perfectly against the sloping roof, screwed into place at every edge. He returned to the owl and examined the wood beneath his feet more closely. Small indentions in the plywood, clearly engraved but unmarked by any contrasting paint, lined the wood beneath the owl's talons. As Reed leaned in closer, he recognized the familiar outlines of Greek letters, but these weren't the letters of a fraternity name—they formed a full sentence, written in ancient Greek.

Reed searched the internet on his phone for an ancient Greek translator, and it didn't take long to find a website that claimed to translate text instantly. Reed painstakingly matched each letter to the Greek alphabet. Beneath his feet, the music continued to pound while college kids laughed and shouted at one another.

He was ten letters in, with another ten to go, when he heard the first scream, shrill and panicked, coming from the front of the house. Reed's back went rigid as the first shout was joined by a second, then a third. Gunshots—fast and chattering—blazed into the house. Heavy thuds sounded beneath him, followed by doors slamming, more screams, and more gunshots.

Banks.

Reed started toward the hole in the ceiling, then stopped, knowing this might be his last chance to get into the attic. Whatever secrets were formed in this dark, strange place led to the deaths of Mitch Holiday and Frank Morccelli. The men behind this blood-eyed owl burned Kelly alive, and he had to know who they were.

Back at the wall, Reed frantically tapped each letter into the phone. Sweat pooled on the LED screen, making his thumbs slip. More gunshots ripped through the house, and two stray bullets blasted through the plywood a few feet to his right.

The last letters clicked into the translator, and Reed tapped the blue button. Seconds dragged by, scraping against his nerves and feeling like hours. The translation loaded, and Reed squinted at the words, whispering the convoluted stream of text back to himself. *"Our mother wisdom war conquest guard secrets beneath mighty feet."*

Reed stepped back and shone the light upward. The owl glared at him, bending invisible menace against his every move. The hellfire that burned in those red eyes spoke of outrage at the broken peace of this strange place.

It was a dark soul eager to protect the secrets that Reed so desperately needed to uncover.

Reed eyed the owl. "Who's the mother?" he demanded. The painted bird didn't respond, but Reed imagined he could see renewed wrath in its scowl.

Reed snapped and slammed his hand against the wall. "Who *is* she?" His forehead collided with the wood, and he pressed his fingers against the carvings, retracing them.

The owl. The mother. Wisdom. War. Conquest.

Reed lifted his head and placed his hand on the face of the bird. The realization sank in, tearing through his mind like a thunderclap.

Owl. Mother. The goddess, Athena.

22

Reed's boots hit the floor of the second-level hallway at the same moment his pistol cleared the holster. At the top of the stairs stood a man dressed in black, wielding an MP5 submachine gun. A black ski mask covered his face, but blue eyes glinted behind it. Reed raised his SIG and fired twice, driving two 9mm slugs right between his eyes. The gunman dropped, but gunshots and screams from the first floor continued. Reed dashed toward the stairs, shoving the handgun in his pocket before snatching up the larger MP5.

At the bottom of the stairs, bullet holes decorated the walls and banister, and outside, the screams of fleeing college kids filled the air. Music continued to pound from the living room, now joined by the flash of disco lights.

Banks screamed again, and this time, Reed could make out her location. He crashed around the end of the banister and charged into the kitchen.

A man pressed Banks against the wall with a handgun jammed into her temple. He screamed at her, "Where's The Prosecutor?"

Banks kicked out with both legs, then spat in his face.

"Hey, you!" Reed screamed. "I'm right here."

The man released Banks and spun toward Reed, the gaping mouth of his weapon following. Reed pressed the trigger of the MP5. The gun fired twice, sending slugs whizzing past the man's arm before it clicked back over an empty magazine. Reed rolled to the floor as a heavy bullet whistled over his head. The MP5 clattered against the hardwood, and he fought for the handgun stuck in his pocket.

The mouth of the gun swung toward Reed. He kicked out with both legs, slamming his boots into the unprotected shins of the gunman. The handgun barked, and hardwood exploded into splinters next to Reed's head. The SIG still lay buried in Reed's pocket, but he managed to force his hand around the grip and reach the trigger. Without aiming, he pushed the muzzle away from his thigh and fired. A bullet rocketed out of his pants and struck the staggering gunman in the ankle. Another scream filled the kitchen, and Reed's attacker stumbled back. Before the masked man could regain his balance, Banks appeared from the back of the kitchen, a can of soup clenched between her fingers. She drove the makeshift weapon full force into the face of the gunman, and he crumpled to the ground as blood gushed from his mask.

Reed pulled himself to his feet as Banks delivered another blow to the top of her attacker's head, but it wasn't necessary. He was out cold already.

"There's more of them outside," Banks said. Fear plagued her eyes, but her voice remained calm.

"Through the front!" Reed shouted.

They crashed over piles of shattered bottles and abandoned cups, sliding through the door as fresh gunfire erupted from the front yard. The windows that framed either side of the door exploded and Reed grabbed Banks, crashing onto the front porch. She slipped and hit the planks with a muted cry. Reed slid to his knees beside her, raising the SIG and opening fire on the gunman. Three pops of the pistol silenced the MP5, and Reed pulled Banks upright.

"Quick, the car!"

They jumped down the porch steps and around the van. The screams continued from the shadows, and fresh gunfire erupted from behind them, back toward the house. Reed emptied the SIG into the home, sending bullets flying at random. The submachine gunfire ceased, and Reed grabbed Banks by the hand.

"Let's go! He's not dead."

Banks gasped for breath and slouched against his arm as they ran. He could feel the exhaustion and the weight of her disease sucking the life out of her and weakening her every step. She pressed on, one foot dragging over the street as they approached the Camaro. Reed slung the passenger door open and pushed her inside. As he jumped into the driver's seat he saw shadows moving inside the frat house, and somebody shouted in a harsh, east European language.

Panic and confusion clouded his mind. *Where the hell did these guys come from?*

The big engine roared to life, and Reed slammed the shifter into first. "Hold on to something!" he shouted, then dumped the clutch. The thunder of the motor was joined by the whine of the supercharger, and the back wheels lost traction. Tire smoke filled the air as the back end of the car fishtailed to the left, and then the tires caught, slinging them into the seats and causing Reed's skull to smack against the headrest. By the time the man in black stepped into the street, it was much too late for him to move. The Camaro launched forward like a rocket, hurtling down the road with the front end lifted an inch off the ground. Banks screamed a split second before the bumper collided with the gunman, sending him tumbling over the hood and back into the street. The front tires slammed against the pavement as Reed jerked the wheel to the right and pulled the emergency brake. The car spun a full one-hundred-eighty degrees, facing the way it had come. Police cars filled the street two hundred yards away, their blue lights ablaze as sirens screamed, and the supercharger whined again.

"Reed, don't do it!"

"Buckle up!"

The police cars swerved to either side as the Camaro screamed down the street like a cannonball. By the time the first car flashed past Reed's window, the heads-up display in the windshield read 63 miles per hour. Nothing he had ever driven compared to the raw power of the supercharged LS motor. Every imperfection in the road sent shudders through the car's tight suspension, though muted by the growl of the motor. A stop sign flashed on the right, and a horn blared. Twenty yards ahead, Reed cut the wheel to the left and redirected toward West End Avenue.

"I found it!" he shouted.

Banks clung to the armrest with wide, panicked eyes, sucking in air between blue lips and screaming as Reed swerved around a taxi.

"It wasn't a fraternity," Reed said. "It was some secret cult. They worshipped the Greek goddess Athena. I saw it all."

He relaxed off the accelerator as the Camaro merged into traffic, and the rearview mirror displayed nothing but an empty avenue behind him. The car shook as the tachometer dropped, but the exhaust still voiced the suspended power ready to be unleashed. Reed wiped the sweat from his forehead and turned abruptly off the road into a large park on the far side of West End. Tall trees overhung a curving road that wound past war memorials and small ponds.

Banks clutched the door handle and peered into the rearview mirror. "We have to go, Reed. They'll find us here. We're not far enough away!"

Reed shook his head. "No, we have to get the book. They hid it in the temple."

"What the hell are you talking about? What book? *What temple?*"

The car squeaked to a stop, the engine still rumbling. Reed nodded toward a wide field. Thin fog clung to the grass, shrouding the park in a cemetery-like mood, enveloping the single structure that dominated the middle of the park. *"That* temple."

Fifty yards away sat the towering bulk of the Parthenon. Constructed of sandy-brown concrete and illuminated by soft-yellow lights, the impending mass of the life-sized replica filled the windshield, commanding reverence. Columns lined every side of the temple, supporting a pitched roof rimmed with spikes. It was breathtaking. Monumental. Haunted.

The moment Reed connected the dots between the owl and the mother, everything fell into place. The owl was a Greek symbol—a sacred token of wisdom and conquest, dedicated to the goddess of the ancient Athenians. This goddess—their holy mother—was also the goddess of war, conquest, science, and mathematics. Athena was a virgin, the offspring of the mytho-logical deity Zeus, and her home was the Parthenon—the temple built for her in the ancient city of Athens.

The concrete building that filled the windshield of the Camaro was a full-scale replica originally designed and constructed in 1897, and had sat in the Centennial Park of Nashville ever since.

Reed knew what was inside. He remembered it all from an eighth-grade field trip when Mountain Brook High School bussed his entire history class to Nashville to tour the Greek monument and learn about Athenian mythology. The featured experience of the trip had been the dominating forty-two-foot-tall statue of Athena herself. It was nothing short of glorious. And it was exactly the place where a cult obsessed with the mother of warfare and wisdom would hide their secret records.

"What is that?" Banks asked. "Is that a government building?"

"You could say that. For a government that died two thousand years ago. We have to get inside."

Banks shook her head. "No, we have to leave. *Now.* They're coming!"

Reed put his foot on the brake. "Banks, this is our best chance of finding them. Those men are just hired guns. Do you want to keep fighting the minions, or do you want to cut the head off the snake?"

Banks looked over her shoulder, back toward Vanderbilt. She licked sweat off her lip, then nodded once. "Okay. Let's hurry."

Reed released the clutch and put his hand on the shifter. He piloted the car around another curve in the asphalt path, weaving toward the parking lot at the main entrance. The closer they drew, the grander the temple appeared. It blocked out the moon, casting a shadow over them as deep and dark as the emptiness Reed felt. He stopped and craned his neck back. Above the tops of the columns, a row of masterfully carved figurines clung to the wall. Gods and goddesses, riding chariots and horses, jutted toward the sky. Their faces were vacant, again speaking to the deadly mystery that led Reed to this strange place.

They were here—Mitch and Frank. Whatever terrible secret cost them their lives, this place was a part of it. This place birthed the monster that killed Kelly.

Reed looked away from the carvings and down the stairs leading beneath the parking lot to the museum's entrance. "We'll only have a few minutes. I won't have time to disarm the alarm systems, so we have to assume that the police will dispatch immediately. Hopefully, the shooting will distract them."

Banks nodded, and sweat dripped from her nose.

He attempted to hold her hand, but she recoiled and shot him an icy glare.

"You ready?" he asked.

She wiped the sweat from her face and slung the door open. "Might as well be. Let's move, shithead."

23

The granite steps that led toward twin glass doors were slick beneath his shoes. Banks limped along on bare feet, her heels abandoned in the car. Her skin rippled with goosebumps, but she didn't complain. Reed felt the irresistible urge to wrap her in a hug, warm her body, and soothe her tired mind. But Banks didn't want comfort. She wanted justice, and it was time to find it.

Reed pushed the mental tumult away and stopped at the doors. A quick press against the handle confirmed they were locked. He pressed his face to the glass and noted an open lobby with restrooms on the left, a gift shop on the right, and beyond that, stairs leading toward the museum.

"Once we breach the doors, we have to move directly to the statue," he said.

"What statue?"

"There's a statue of Athena in the main temple room. When we were in that house, I found a script etched into the attic wall beneath a carving of an owl. The owl is one of Athena's symbols, and the script said secrets were housed beneath her feet—beneath the statue."

Banks shot him a glare. "Are you serious? We're breaking into a museum based on an owl and something whittled into a wall?"

Reed started to object, then stopped. "Yes," he said. "That's pretty much what's happening."

Banks looked back toward the university, then waved at the door. "Well, hurry!"

Reed pulled the SIG from his belt and checked the magazine. Four weeks ago, he possessed a collection of small arms sufficient to knock down a National Guard post. Now, only the backup handgun and the three bullets it contained stood between him and the army of gunmen on his tail.

Life's a bitch.

He pointed the little gun at the glass and pulled the trigger. Glass exploded, and only milliseconds later, the shrill ring of an alarm ripped through the air. Reed drove his boot through what remained of the door, sending a cascade of glass clattering against the granite. He jammed his hand through the hole and flipped the latch, then pushed the door open.

Banks jumped onto his back, wrapping her arms around his neck as her bare feet swung over the shards of razor-sharp glass. Reed rushed past the gift shop and pounded up the steps. The pressure of her arms against his bruised and cut neck blinded his mind with pain and restricted his airflow. He leaned against the wall, and Banks slid off, her feet smacking the smooth tile floor.

Dim light illuminated glass display boxes full of Greek artifacts and replicas. As they circled the tight halls and topped another set of steps, the blare of the alarm grew louder, bouncing against the walls and shrieking in their ears. Two more flights of stairs through more display cases and art galleries, and they burst through a door, skidding to a halt at the entrance of the main temple.

Even though he'd seen it before, the mass of the statue sent a shiver down his spine. It was all at once majestic and terrifying. On a raised platform in the middle of the giant hall, with columns on all sides, Athena wore a golden robe hanging from her white marble shoulders and draping down over her feet. A golden war helmet rested over her head, gleaming above piercing blue eyes.

She held the statue of an angel in her outstretched right hand, and a massive shield adorned with Greek art leaned against her left thigh. Between her left knee and the shield, a serpent reared its golden head, glaring out at them as they stood twenty feet away, staring back at the horrifying and magnificent recreation of Greek worship.

"My God . . ." Banks whispered.

Reed was jarred out of his stupor by the continued blare of the alarm. He shook his head to clear it, then pushed Banks toward the steps that led down to the main floor. "We have to hurry."

The statue was encircled by red velvet rope, and Reed clicked his flashlight on and scanned the pedestal beneath Athena's massive feet, where golden, mid-relief sculptures projected from the base. They were Greek characters—peasants, gods, warriors, all crafted in painstaking detail.

"What are we looking for?" Banks asked.

"I don't know. Something hidden. The script said the secrets were housed beneath her feet. That could mean directly under her shoes or anywhere in the platform."

Banks slid on her knees along the far side of the dais as Reed worked between the golden figurines of warriors, poets, and rulers standing in a tight row, wielding spears and riding horses. He moved his fingers against their feet and between their bodies, searching for any crack or hidden script—anything that might house the secret of a thirty-year-old cult.

"Reed! Come here!"

Banks shouted from the rear of the platform, and Reed hurried around the back corner. Over the alarm that shrieked overhead, he thought he could hear distant police sirens growing gradually closer, but there was no way to tell if they were headed for the Parthenon or the shooting scene on campus.

Banks knelt in the middle of the platform, where she pressed her fingers against a small symbol hidden between the legs of a horse. Reed saw the light of discovery in her eyes.

"It's an owl," she said.

Reed knelt beside her, shining the light on the dime-size spot nestled so far toward the horse's protruding chest that the only way to see it was to kneel. Etched in red ink, the clear outline of an owl's face, painted in reflective paint, glowed under his flashlight. Reed ran his finger over the carving, making out its rough texture. He pushed in, but the owl didn't move.

"What is it?" she whispered. "Can you feel anything?"

He shook his head and felt around the hooves and neck of the horse, searching for a crack or crevice—anything that moved or shifted.

"Wait," Banks said. "Didn't you say she was the goddess of wisdom?"

"Yeah. Why?"

"The scribe." Banks motioned to the figurine of a Greek man dressed in soft robes. He didn't wear armor, and unlike the others, he didn't carry a weapon. Held between his hands was a thick, gold scroll—the symbol of knowledge and understanding.

Reed wrapped his fingers around the scroll, pulling out, but feeling nothing. He twisted, and a dull click resounded from behind the stone. As he continued pulling on the scroll, the scribe shuddered, and dust fell from around the figurine's head and shoulders. It slid outward, grinding against the stone, then fell away from the platform, displaying a guide rod sticking out of his back that corresponded with a hole in the stone. Set in a cavity just beneath the hole was a small leather notebook with a red-eyed silver owl printed on the cover.

"That's it!" Reed hissed. He jerked the book out and ran his hands over the leather. Banks shoved the scribe back in place and twisted his scroll into the locked position while Reed pried dry rubber bands off the notebook.

"What is it? What does it say?" Banks hissed.

Reed shook his head and turned to the first page. It was covered in Greek symbols, filling every open space right up to the edges. He flipped a few more, exposing black-and-white pictures, all taken inside the attic of the frat house. He recognized the owl with the red eyes, and even though all the figures in each image wore black robes and full masks, he thought he recognized Mitch Holiday by his broad shoulders and thick neck—the frame of a running back.

Each photo depicted a ceremony. A table, covered in blood, was set up beneath the talons of the owl, and parts of various animals—rabbits, cats, a few birds—lay on the floor, all dismembered with their intestines strewn about amid the feet of the robed worshipers.

"What the hell?" Banks whispered. "Is that Greek worship?"

Reed shook his head. "Not like any I've ever read about. This is something else entirely."

He flipped two more pages, then stopped at an entry written in red ink. Unlike previous entries, these letters formed English words he could clearly read.

Under the sacred eye of our mother, we pledge ourselves to her worship. We, the holy members of this sect, protectors of wisdom, embracers of conquest, warriors of the world, commit our lives to her service, and our bodies to this brotherhood. From end to end.

Reed glided his finger down the page, tracing a short list of biographies. Banks leaned in closer, her breath warm against his neck. His finger stopped at Mitchell Holiday, followed almost immediately by Frances Morccelli—names he expected to see. Reed pushed on down the page, skipping over anecdotes about Frank and Mitch's involvement, searching for the list of remaining members. He flipped the page and felt his heart stop. His vision blurred around the next name and he blinked himself back into focus. His fingers went numb, and the notebook slipped from his hand, clattering to the floor amid a confused gasp from Banks. She snatched the book up and flicked her way back to the page, holding it under the light. After a moment, she shut the book and turned toward Reed, her lips pressed into a demanding frown.

Reed looked away, trying to shut out the flood of questions pouring into his tired mind. There was no denying the clean handwriting on that page and no refuting the name written there. It was a name he knew all too well, and one he hadn't heard in years, but it was a name he would never forget.

David Montgomery.

24

"It's your father, isn't it? David Montgomery?"

Reed nodded but avoided her gaze. "Yes."

She grabbed him by the chin, wrenching his face toward her, and her voice snapped. "Did you know? Is this why we met? Why you kidnapped my godfather?"

"I had no idea!" He jerked away. "I barely knew my father. I haven't seen him in two decades. I don't—"

Gunshots cracked from outside. Men screamed, and a shotgun boomed.

Reed snatched the book back and crammed it into his cargo pocket, then hoisted Banks to her feet. "Let's go!"

He cast one more glance at the back of the statue, watching the dust drift through the air around the war helmet.

My father stood here. My father was a part of this.

They ran back up the steps, through the art gallery and the back of the museum. The gift shop flashed past on their right as they pounded through the lobby and toward the door. Banks swung from his shoulders again as he crunched over the glass, and blue police lights flashed through the shattered front door. Gunshots still popped from the park, and as they climbed the steps back to ground level, Reed's foot collided with a body. A METRO cop lay on the concrete, bleeding out as his hands twitched at his sides.

Reed dropped Banks and slid to his knees beside the officer, feeling for a pulse against the man's neck. "Can you hear me?"

The cop's gaze drifted toward him, but he didn't respond. Reed searched beneath the blue shirt until his fingers touched the wound. The bullet had passed just below the ribcage.

Two gunshots ripped through the air, and the edge of the sidewalk exploded into a cloud of concrete dust only inches from Reed's knee. He snatched up the cop's service pistol and directed it toward the trees, unleashing a string of shots at random.

"Banks! Get him down the steps. He can't be hit again!"

Banks grabbed the officer by his ankles and dragged him out of the line of fire as Reed turned toward the smoking hulk of a squad car twenty feet away. Bullet holes riddled the rear fender, and the back glass was blown out. Another cop, holding his side, lay against the sheltered side of the car, a bloody shotgun on the ground next to him.

Reed lifted the cop's sagging head. Faint breaths were warm against his hand, but the tension in the policeman's body was obvious.

"Stay with me, officer."

"I was going to get married," he whispered.

Reed ripped his shirt off and tore it into strips, searching the officer's body for the source of the blood. He found two gunshot wounds, both in the gut. Under the glint of the moon, he made out the officer's nameplate— B. Friz. That was a good name, he thought. The kind of name that didn't take itself too seriously.

"Listen here, Officer Friz. You're gonna marry that girl. You hear me? We're gonna get you home."

Reed wrapped the strips around Friz's middle, but even as he pressed against the wound, he could feel the life slipping away. Friz's arms fell against the concrete, and Reed withdrew from the body, searching for a pulse around his wrist, then his neck.

"No . . . Friz. Stay with me, dammit!"

Banks stumbled up beside him, blood coating her hands and smeared across her face. "Reed . . . the other cop. He's gone. I didn't know what to do."

The ache that descended over Reed felt more like a fog than any conscious pain. A distant agony of a traumatic injury muted by morphine, but still there, ripping through his heart. He slammed his hand into the side of the car and screamed.

Gunshots rang again, and Banks grabbed his shoulder. "Reed, we have to do something!"

Sirens screamed in the distance. It was the voice of more officers rushing into the jaws of death to protect people they might not even know.

Their blood is on my hands.

The thunder of a shotgun jarred Reed from his daze.

Banks leaned over the hood of the car, directing Friz's gun toward the trees. She pumped another shell into the chamber and fired again, felling limbs and spraying dead leaves across the grounds.

We have to run. We can't win if we stay here.

Shadows flitted through the darkness. Muzzle flash illuminated the space between the trees, and a shower of small-arms fire skipped over the pavement and slammed into the squad car. Banks covered her head and curled into a fetal position.

Reed grabbed Banks by the arm, pulling her behind the shelter of the patrol car just as more bullets tore over the hood. "We've got to get to the car! Come on, Banks. You've got to run now."

A brief pause in the gunfire brought welcome relief to the chaos, but the police car's siren and the alarms from the Parthenon still blared. Reed lifted Banks off the ground. She felt limp in his arms, and her skin was clammy, a now-familiar sign of her disease taking over.

She's almost done.

He hoisted her over his shoulder and sprinted toward the Camaro fifty yards away. Gunfire resumed behind him, bullets skipping against the pavement around his feet. One of them tore the toe of his boot, missing his toes by millimeters. Reed ducked and wove, jerking erratically back and forth as the gunfire intensified. His saving grace was the inherent inaccuracy of a pistol-caliber submachine gun fired in full auto mode. At a hundred yards, his chances of evading the scathing fire were about as good as being cut down by it.

His lungs were ready to collapse as he ground to a halt next to the Camaro. Banks hung limp in his arms, her strength fading. He opened the passenger's door and set her inside, locking the seat belt in place before he slid across the front hood of the car.

A blast of gunfire chattered against a Confederate memorial statue sheltering the Camaro. Reed cursed and dug the SIG from his pocket, unleashing his final two rounds. The puny pop of the handgun was insufficient to defy the fully automatic bursts, inaccurate though they were.

The shadows of two men began their approach. Reed slung open the driver's door and piled inside. Banks clutched the handle and groaned, and her head twitched.

"Hang on, Banks. We're getting out of here."

Reed shifted into first and stomped on the gas. An unearthly bellow burst from the engine, the familiar thunder of the big V-8 mixed with the whine of the supercharger. Both rear tires squealed, and the car launched out of the parking lot. Reed swung the wheel to the left, and the back end of the vehicle pivoted outward, sending clouds of tire smoke and bits of asphalt shooting into the air.

The two gunmen in the shadows—masked, tall, and wielding submachine guns—were now joined by a third. The Camaro hurtled straight toward them, leaping a speed bump and slicing through the parking lot with no sign of stopping. A panicked shout rose from the lead gunman, and he dove out of the way just in time to miss the car. Reed jerked back to the right and slid toward West End, slapping the shifter into second. Headlights flashed behind him, and a black pickup truck with fog lights mounted over the roof barreled out of the trees. Its motor howled, and he recognized the whine of a supercharger.

Shit.

Sweat coated the steering wheel, and his hands trembled as he worked the shifter and dumped the clutch, swerving around a garbage truck and whistling through a red light. Businesses, restaurants, and parked cars blurred around him as the Camaro kept climbing past eighty miles an hour. The truck was only a quarter mile behind and barreling toward him.

A green sign ahead displayed an arrow pointing to the right: 440 WEST. *They won't keep up on the highway.*

Banks groaned, and her head rolled toward him. He placed one hand on her neck, bracing her as he swerved in front of a sedan and turned toward the on-ramp. Darkness clung around the road, shrouding his view. Yards away from the ramp, a stopped car in the middle of the road came into view. It blocked his path onto the highway as its flashers blinked a steady rhythm of yellow. Reed shouted and jerked the Camaro back to the left, hopping over a bump in the road and sliding back onto West End Avenue, still hurtling like a rocket.

He could hear the bellow of his pursuer, even over the howl of the Camaro. There could be no mistake—this guy was going to run him to ground.

"All right, bitch," Reed hissed. "You asked for it."

He downshifted into third and pushed the pedal to the floor. The front end of the car lifted away from the pavement, and every part of the car shuddered, sending shivers through Reed's body. A red light flashed from the dash, alerting him that the car had reached redline. He power-shifted into fourth and clung to the wheel, watching the speedometer pass 110.

"It's not just a car, Reed." Dave Montgomery's distant voice echoed in his mind, a memory from ages gone by. For a moment, the plastic dash and Alcantara trim of the fifth-gen Camaro was replaced by the hard metal and vinyl of Dave Montgomery's 1969 Z/28, and Reed was transported back to his first drag race—the way the car lifted free of the ground as Dave Montgomery slammed his foot into the gas while his eight-year-old son sat in the passenger seat, screaming with joy. *"It's art, son. It's you, the motor, and the open road."*

The blur of Midtown Nashville returned, and Reed clung to the wheel. He ignored the speedometer. Nothing mattered but the open road—this moment between himself, the car . . . and Dave Montgomery.

By the time he saw the bus, it was too late. The intersection loomed directly ahead, a sign reading White Bridge Pike. Small brick buildings clustered together on either side of the street. In the distance, a hospital towered in the sky. Reed saw it all in the same millisecond the long city bus pulled into the intersection, only yards ahead, loaded with a smattering of people sitting behind dirty windows. In the split second it took his mind to register the blocked pathway ahead, his foot was already slipping off the accelerator, colliding with the brake, and pressing toward the floor. The front tires of the Camaro screamed, and the car fishtailed as Reed jammed harder against the brakes, but the vehicle barely slowed. Smoke poured from both front wheels as the brake pads ground and slipped against the rotors.

"Watch out for the brakes. They're too small for this much power." The mechanic's warning about the Camaro's undersized brakes echoed in his mind a moment too late.

The bus flashed closer, and the world slowed around him as he made eye contact with a passenger in the rear of the bus, her grey hair pulled back in a ponytail, eyes filled with terror as she saw the car rocketing toward her like a cannonball. Reed snatched the emergency brake and jerked the wheel, sending the car spinning toward a wall of buildings.

25

The moment before the Camaro made contact was one Reed would never forget. Even though he wasn't looking at Banks, he saw her face as clearly as the first night they met. Her shining eyes, the bright smile, every gorgeous thing he loved so much about her, right beside him.

The Camaro collided with a tree first. The rear bumper of the car crashed against the towering oak, and a shower of metal ripped across the pavement as the car skidded across the sidewalk. A fire hydrant exploded, and glass rained down around them. The air was alive with the odor of burnt rubber and oil, and the seatbelt cinched down around Reed's neck. He reached out for Banks as the Camaro continued spinning, bouncing off a retaining wall, and hurtling toward another tree.

The hood of the car popped upward, and both airbags blasted into the interior of the car. Everything descended into a daze of crunched metal and smoke as the car finally screeched to a stop, and Reed pried his hands free of the steering wheel. His ears rang. Everything around him danced in a confused blur, and through the haze he heard his own voice calling for Banks. But he couldn't see her.

Fire erupted from the engine bay, and the reek of burning carpet filled his nostrils. He clawed at the seatbelt, clicking it free of the latch, and slammed his shoulder into the bent door of the car—once, twice. On the third strike, the door swung open, and Reed spilled out onto the concrete, gasping for air.

Where's Banks?

Panic overtook his mind, and he was vaguely aware of streetlights glimmering around him as people shouted. But none of that mattered. He stumbled back toward the car as flames continued building in the engine compartment, licking their way toward the gas tank at the rear of the car.

My God, no. Don't take her.

He slid around the rear of the car and reached the passenger's door, crunched together and impossibly distorted. He slammed his unprotected fist into what remained of the window, clearing out the shards of glass. Banks lay inside, slumped forward with a trail of blood dripping from her forehead. Reed leaned through the window and fumbled with the seatbelt, clicking it free as black smoke clouded his eyes. He could hear the roar of the pickup truck now, hurtling down the avenue half a mile away.

"Banks, come on. You've got to help me!"

Her head twitched, and she turned toward him. Her face was covered in soot, and her body so weak she could barely hold her head up, but she wriggled toward the window. Reed leaned back and pulled, clearing her shoulders of the window frame, then her stomach. The car shuddered against his efforts as flames filled the cabin. A cry of pain erupted from her swollen lips, and they crashed to the pavement. Heat flooded his face, singeing his hair as smoke clogged his throat. Banks lay on top of him, limp and unconscious, but breathing.

"Don't let go," he whispered. "I need you. God help me, I need you."

The truck behind him screamed to a halt, and three men dressed in black, wearing ski masks and wielding submachine guns, piled out. They stomped toward him in slow motion, the smoke of the car fire drifting around their tall frames and making them appear ghostly, like the villains of a slasher movie.

Reed choked for air and rolled over, stumbling to his feet and clawing for the SIG. He knew the gun was empty, but somehow pointing it at the oncoming killers still felt better than giving up. Snot drained from his nose as his lungs continued to flood with acidic smoke. The three men drew closer, closing the gap between the truck and the burning car. The lead man was shorter than the rest, and under the ski mask, Reed made out the dark tinge of olive skin. He wrapped his finger around the trigger of his gun, raised the weapon, and trained it on Reed.

Reed released the SIG, abandoning it in his pocket, then took a step forward, placing himself between the gunman and Banks. Everything slowed around him. Smoke drifted from his lips as he breathed out, exhaling the smog from the car fire. He stared into those dark eyes, and for a moment, the world grew still.

This is it. This is how it ends.

The glare of lights and the roar of a motor burst through the stillness. A split second of confusion flashed across the dark gaze of the gunman, and he turned toward the sound as a Mercedes coupe rushed toward them. The bumper of the big car rammed through the two rear gunmen, shattering their bodies in an instant and sending their guns flying.

Even before the car stopped, the driver's side door flung open. Wolfgang appeared in all black, his giant Glock 10mm pistol swinging from one hand. But he didn't turn toward Reed. He turned toward the short, olive-skinned man.

The gunman raised his weapon and clawed at the trigger, spraying shots around the scene of carnage. Wolfgang's giant handgun thundered, spitting a bullet through the smoke, and the slug crashed through the gunman's shoulder. The weapon fell from the man's fingers as he screamed and crashed to the pavement. Wolfgang followed him, shoving right past Reed and snatching his victim off the pavement with one powerful arm. Reed watched as The Wolf pivoted on his heel and slammed the gunman against the side of the Mercedes. With a quick flip of his fingers, the ski mask was ripped away, exposing the brown features and terrified eyes of the face beneath.

It was Salvador. Reed would have recognized that panicked face anywhere. The face of the man who kidnapped Banks, threatened Reed over the phone, and was the author of the fallout in Atlanta. Salvador, the only definite link between Reed and the shadowy men who wanted Mitchell Holiday assassinated.

Wolfgang shoved the mass of the Glock into Salvador's throat and snarled in his face.

"No!" Reed shouted. "I need him!"

Reed jumped over the bodies and rushed toward the truck, his mind pounding in a confusing swirl of desperation. Every step was agony, as though he were dragging himself through quicksand. Wolfgang's words warbled and echoed, distorted by Reed's frayed consciousness and pounding head.

"*Where is she?*"

Salvador shook, and Wolfgang backhanded him, shattering his nose and sending blood streaming over his lip. "Where is my sister?"

Salvador's eyes were bloodshot and draining tears, his face reddened under another brutal blow from The Wolf, but he didn't speak. The muzzle of the gun was jammed harder into his throat, closing off his windpipe.

"*Collins!*" Wolfgang roared. "Where is she?"

Reed slid to a stop and clawed at the gun in his pocket. It finally tore free of his pants, and he raised it, directing the muzzle toward The Wolf. "Wolfgang!" he gasped. "Don't do it. I need him to talk!"

Wolfgang glanced at Reed. Their eyes met, and fire clashed against fire. For a moment, Reed thought he might redirect the Glock away from Salvador and toward him—The Wolf's original target. Instead, he ignored Reed and turned back to the South American.

"Kill The Prosecutor," Salvador hissed. "And I'll tell you."

Wolfgang sneered and wrapped his finger around the trigger of the pistol. "If you wanted him dead, you should have never touched my sister."

The Glock swung downward, then thundered. Blood exploded from Salvador's thigh, and Reed started forward.

"Don't kill him. I need to know who he's working for!"

"*Stay back, Montgomery!*" Wolfgang swept the gun toward Reed, stopping him in his tracks. Salvador writhed in pain, trying to collapse against the concrete, but Wolfgang held him suspended against the car.

"I can do this all night." Wolfgang breathed malice over Salvador, placing the gun back against his stomach. "Where's my sister?"

Salvador coughed, spitting up saliva. "She's in an apartment . . . Detroit . . . Oak Ridge Place . . . unit B7. She's safe, I swear."

Wolfgang dropped Salvador and raised the barrel of the oversized handgun.

Reed rushed forward. "Don't!"

The pistol thundered, and Salvador's face exploded in a spray of blood. Reed stood over the dead South American, his hand trembling as he lowered the empty SIG. He stared down at the crumpled body and felt desperation take over. It blocked out his fear and panic, and nothing but defeat filled his mind.

Wolfgang stood next to him, staring down at the body, then spat onto the corpse. He turned toward Reed, and for a moment, neither one spoke. The soft breeze that swept over the crime scene carried the stench of blood and sweat and burning rubber. The Camaro burst into a total blaze as gasoline ignited, boiling the air around them.

"I'm sorry, Montgomery," Wolfgang said. "We all have rules. He broke mine."

"I needed him *alive!*" Reed snapped. "Who hired you to kill me?"

Wolfgang looked back down at the body and motioned with the gun. "He did."

Once again, the silence descended around them, broken only by the crackle of the flames. Reed raised his gun, pointing it toward The Wolf. "You said you were going to kill me next time we met. I can't let you do that."

Wolfgang stared down the barrel of the gun to the blackened face of The Prosecutor. His finger relaxed around the trigger of his own gun, then he holstered it.

"It's after midnight," he muttered. "Good luck, Montgomery."

Without another word, Wolfgang turned back toward his car. The big German motor roared to life, tires howled against the pavement, and the coupe rocketed away into the darkness.

Reed slumped to the ground and rested his face in his hands. His body racked with dry sobs as the gun toppled to the ground beside him. The stench of blood that filled his nostrils was so familiar now, he didn't even notice it. He didn't recognize the carnage, or the chaos, or the death that hung around him like a cloak. The wreckage of war. And yet, at this moment, the weight of it all crashed down on him like a load of bricks.

Footsteps tapped on the pavement, soft and slow. Banks staggered toward him, clutching herself and pinning the burned and tattered clothes to her body as she surveyed the carnage with a blank face. She stopped a few feet away, then picked up his fallen gun.

The ache returned to Reed's chest, piling on to the defeat he already felt. "Are you going to kill me now?"

Banks looked down at the gun, then frowned. Her voice was weak and cracked. "What are you talking about? We've still got work to do."

Reed motioned toward Salvador's body. "He's dead, Banks. He's gone. Whoever he worked for . . . they're lost now. Another shadow."

She gazed at the mutilated corpse for a moment, then turned back to Reed. "And what about David Montgomery?"

A knot tightened in Reed's stomach. The name ripped through his heart and shattered every reality he had carefully constructed over the last nineteen years, every lie he ever crafted to forget the man who was his father.

"He's alive," he whispered.

"And you know where he is?"

Reed closed his eyes, then nodded slowly. "I do."

"On your feet, then. This isn't over yet."

The gun clicked, and Reed opened his eyes to see Banks's outstretched hand. Her face was still damp, and her fingers trembled, but there was steel in her eyes. Relentless resolve.

"I'll let you know when you can quit, Reed Montgomery."

Reed felt the blood return to his head. He pulled himself to his feet and caught her just in time to keep Banks from collapsing. She huddled close to his chest as he cradled her in his arms and stumbled toward the pickup truck. In the distance, the ever-present howl of sirens roared toward them. He cast a look around the blood and bodies piled near the truck. There was no way to hide the massacre, so there was only one option left. Keep running.

He laid Banks into the passenger seat of the truck, then hauled himself in behind the wheel. In the distance, locals gathered around the stopped bus, watching with gaping mouths. They would need therapy. After tonight, a lot of people would need therapy—one of the many costs of the bloodshed. But that didn't change the inevitability of it all. There was no other choice, no other way out of the twisted hell he found himself in. Salvador might be dead, but it was now clear how trivial a tool Salvador really was—a minion of a much larger villain still hidden in the shadows. The secrets he unearthed in the Parthenon would cost a great deal more blood before this was over.

More than that, it was personal now—more personal than Banks or Oliver could have ever made it. It wasn't about avenging the woman he used to love, or protecting the woman he would always love—now it was about him.

David Montgomery was there when this evil was born, and Reed Montgomery would be there when it died.

26

Gambit could feel the twist of tension in his stomach and the dampness on his palms. His feet dragged over the carpet in spite of his efforts to walk normally. With each step toward the elevator, the weight on his shoulders grew heavier.

He mashed the button for the fiftieth floor and adjusted his tie. There was no one else in the elevator. In fact, at three in the morning, there were very few people inside the skyscraper at all. Other than cleaning crews and security guards, the hallways lay empty, lending a haunted aura to the giant building.

As each floor ticked by, Gambit fingered the sleeve of his custom-tailored suit and reviewed what he planned to say. Would it be best to lead with the Montgomery situation or discuss Governor Trousdale? He wanted to remain in control of the conversation—provide solutions, not problems. In his line of work, he found that people who provided problems found themselves out of a job, if they were lucky. The unlucky ones wound up six feet under.

The bell dinged, and the gold doors of the elevator rolled open. Gambit straightened his back. He screwed up, and he wasn't going to deny that. Now he had to fix it.

Scarlet carpet lined the hallway. Gambit had traveled this path a thousand times, so much so that it felt more like home than his own penthouse. And yet, the grandeur of the fiftieth-floor suite still made him question his belonging. It was imposter syndrome at its worst. Gambit placed his hand on the gold handle, cleared his throat, and pushed inside.

The suite, complete with the scent of lavender and vanilla, was expansive, filling half of the fiftieth floor. Massive windows looked southward toward the heart of downtown. A minibar sat on one side of the room, and a massive executive desk on the other. Filling the space in between were lounge chairs and a chess table with ivory pieces standing five inches tall. Otherwise the room was bare, and sterile, reflecting the economic tastes of the man facing the skyline with his back toward Gambit. The door slid shut automatically, leaving Gambit standing in the relaxing darkness of the room.

"It's bad, isn't it?" The man standing in front of the glass didn't turn around. Hands folded behind his back, he spoke with perfect calm. His voice carried no edge, no tone, but Gambit knew the power hidden beneath the practiced posture. The venom.

"It's not good," Gambit said. "Things went sideways in Nashville."

"Why the hell was *anything* happening in Nashville?"

Gambit spoke with confidence. "It was Salvador, the man I hired to take care of Mitch Holiday. He made a mess."

"Sounds like it. I've read the news."

Gambit refused to hesitate or display any signs of the anxiety that plagued him. "I'm still collecting intel, but it appears there was a confrontation."

"A confrontation? Is that what you call this slaughter? They killed at least two cops. Montgomery got away. And then there's this Wolf. Somebody Salvador hired, I take it?"

"Salvador got sloppy. I take full responsibility and will ensure that he is removed from the equation."

The man at the window turned around, his hands still folded behind him. He was tall and slim, and with the moon at his back, his appearance was altogether impending. Greying black hair was swept behind large ears, with deep, penetrating eyes the hallmark of his face. He settled down behind the desk before motioning to the minibar. "Whiskey . . . on ice. Fix yourself something."

Gambit hurried to prepare the drink, splashing three fingers of bourbon into a glass for himself. He handed his employer a glass of expensive Irish whiskey, then took a seat.

His boss took a long sip of the drink. "Salvador is already out of the equation."

Gambit frowned. "How do you know?"

"Because Montgomery escaped. He wouldn't have left Salvador alive—not after all the chaos that fool caused. Our priority now is damage control. We're making entirely too much noise. There's already an FBI agent sniffing around—the guy who was hounding Holiday. Now we've got a rogue killer on our hands. Montgomery needs to be on ice, immediately, along with anyone working with him."

"I'll take care of it . . . personally."

"I know you will." The man took a sip of whiskey and met Gambit's gaze. There was ice in his stare—a chill that turned Gambit's stomach.

Gambit coughed and took a swallow of bourbon. "There's another issue. Governor Trousdale. She's going to be a problem."

"I thought you spoke with her."

Gambit nodded. "I did. I leaned on her pretty hard, but she's not budging. She's got this crusade against corruption. It's her whole campaign promise. I think she actually believes in it."

"You know how this game is played. Doesn't she have a family?"

"I tried." Gambit set the glass on the table. "I really think the harder we lean on her, the more she's going to fight back. She needs to be taken out, promptly, before she causes any more noise."

"You want to assassinate the governor of Louisiana?"

"We already sent a gunman after her."

"Only to scare her her into cooperation."

"I know. That backfired, though. She's a fighter, tooth and nail, and I don't think we can break her."

The silver-haired man stared at Gambit a moment, then stood up and gestured toward the chess table. Gambit followed him, feeling the knots in his stomach constrict. He stopped a couple feet away and watched as his boss lifted the white queen and traced the delicate outlines of each carving.

"Stephen, why do I call you Gambit?"

Gambit shifted, then cleared his throat. "Because that's my job. To take risks, implement deceit, and make things happen."

"That's right. And for almost a decade, you've been my most indispensable piece. Honestly, Stephen, this company would not be what it is today without your brilliance, dedication, and ferocity. Your hard work is appreciated more than you'll ever know."

Gambit glanced at the floor. "Thank you. That means a lot."

For a moment, the silence hung in the air, while the man gently stroked the queen, scraping his thumbnail over the polished ivory. "The funny thing is, Stephen, that a career full of highlights and trophies can be undone in a matter of seconds. Just a few critical mistakes. This company is a tower built on a delicate foundation—a foundation that depends on *every* piece."

Gambit felt claws of ice dig into his soul. He remained frozen, rooted to the floor, staring at the chessboard. Waiting for the next words.

The silver-haired man cleared his throat and set the queen down abruptly. It clicked against the marble chessboard.

"I don't want you wasting time lamenting the things you can't change. I want you to do what you do best—make problems go away. If you tell me Governor Trousdale is an irreparable liability, then I trust your judgment. Erase the liability."

"Yes, sir. I'll just need to find a way to keep it out of the headlines."

"She's the governor of Louisiana, Stephen. It's *going* to make headlines. May I make a suggestion?"

Gambit nodded hastily. "Of course."

His boss crossed his arms. "Montgomery is a wanted man suspected of killing a state senator. One could presume that he has a penchant for killing politicians. Perhaps that is because of his bad experiences in the Iraq war. Who knows? Why not use one liability against the other, and kill two birds with one stone?"

Gambit frowned. "You want me to pin the murder of Governor Trousdale on Montgomery?"

"No, I want you to have Montgomery kill her himself, and then make sure the FBI finds out about it."

Gambit tried not to grimace. "He's impossible to manage, sir. Salvador attempted to manipulate him by kidnapping Holiday's goddaughter, and it all blew up. I don't think we can force him to kill anyone."

Gambit's boss lifted the black king off the chessboard and set it in the middle. Slowly, he began to rearrange the white pieces, aligning them around the black king. "Stephen, I shouldn't have to tell you this. Everything is a matter of positioning. You place your subject alone"—he adjusted the black king in the center of the board, then placed a white rook within striking distance and a knight blocking the retreat—"then you surround him. Give him no other way out. Salvador screwed up because Salvador grabbed a tiger by the tail. You're never going to get that close. Drive Montgomery into a corner, and then open up a single route of escape—over Governor Trousdale's dead body. Don't tell him what to do. Just leave him no other option."

Gambit's eyes gleamed with excitement. "Do I use the girl?"

"No. You'll need more than that. Something that reaches deeper into his psyche, all the way back to his earliest memories."

Gambit tilted his head, and slowly, a smile spread across his face.

The silver-haired man thumped the black king, knocking it over. "Stephen, it's time we reconnect with an old friend. It's time we brought David Montgomery out of retirement."

SMOKE AND MIRRORS
THE REED MONTGOMERY SERIES Book 4

When killers hide in the shadows, it's time to set the world on fire.

After declaring war on the criminal underworld, elite assassin Reed Montgomery uncovered a crippling secret: The organization he's fighting was founded by his father, and Reed must confront him if he has any hope of defeating it.

Reaching David Montgomery is easier said than done, however. While in prison for manslaughter, insanity has taken hold, and now David doesn't remember his own son.

Armed with a list of his father's known associates, Reed will drive out the truth by any means necessary. But some men will give anything to protect their secrets, and they are every bit as ruthless as Reed.

This war isn't over. It's only just begun.

Get your copy today at
severnriverbooks.com/series/reed-montgomery

ABOUT THE AUTHOR

Logan Ryles was born in small town USA and knew from an early age he wanted to be a writer. After working as a pizza delivery driver, sawmill operator, and banker, he finally embraced the dream and has been writing ever since. With a passion for action-packed and mystery-laced stories, Logan's work has ranged from global-scale political thrillers to small town vigilante hero fiction.

Beyond writing, Logan enjoys saltwater fishing, road trips, sports, and fast cars. He lives with his wife and three fun-loving dogs in Alabama.

Sign up for Logan Ryles's reader list at
severnriverbooks.com/authors/logan-ryles